The Pony Whisperer

THE WORD ON THE YARD

Collect all of The Pony Whisperer books:

The Word on the Yard
Team Challenge

The Pony Whisperer

THE WORD ON THE YARD

JANET RISING

sourcebooks
jabberwocky

Published by Sourcebooks Jabberwocky, an imprint of Sourcebooks, Inc.
P.O. Box 4410, Naperville, Illinois 60567-4410
(630) 961-3900
Fax: (630) 961-2168
www.jabberwockykids.com

First published in Great Britain in 2009 by Hodder Children's Books.

Library of Congress Cataloging-in-Publication data is on file with the publisher.

Source of Production: Versa Press, East Peoria, Illinois, USA
Date of Production: June 2010
Run Number: 12509

Printed and bound in the United States of America.

VP 10 9 8 7 6 5 4 3 2 1

To Rose, with thanks

CHAPTER 1

DRUMMER LOOKED AT ME and sighed. "What am I doing in this dump?" he seemed to say. I knew exactly how he felt. Ever since my mom and I had moved to our new house I had been sighing. A lot. Moving meant that my pony Drummer moved, too—there was no way I was leaving him behind; it was bad enough us both having to leave all our friends! So my mom and I had searched the DIY stables close to our new (teeny-weeny) house and we found one we liked in an old farmyard with a view over what would have been parkland in days gone by, with lovely old trees in the field and cornfields beyond that. With an entrance hidden along a tree-lined track, Laurel Farm was old and full of character with ancient wooden stables and an oak tree in the yard, a lazy brindle greyhound called Squish, assorted cats draped over straw bales and buckets, and a rather crazy woman in charge called Mrs. Collins. She seemed to walk around the yard in her slippers all the time. I don't know why, and I can't say I cared enough to ask.

When we had first visited the yard, it had been a sunny day and there were ponies in the field and in the stables and girls in the yard who seemed to be about my own age. The big news was spying a chestnut mare with a white face being ridden in the outdoor school by a really cute boy—not that that had influenced my choice of stables, you understand. Well, maybe just a little. I mean, he was hot and you don't get many boys, let alone *hot* boys, at stable yards. I decided that if we had to move (and, apparently, we did have to because my dad had moved out of our house and in with his skinny new girlfriend, meaning we had to move to somewhere much, much smaller that Mom could afford by herself), I might as well be at a yard with a hot boy around!

Anyway, it wasn't sunny when I moved Drummer to his new home; it was raining and the yard was dank and wet with puddles everywhere and there was no sign of the hot boy—only rain dripping from the gutters and straw blowing around like trash. *And* I spotted a rat scurrying behind the muck heap. Oh, great, I thought, Drum has pets. It looked like a dump. Plus, all the other ponies were out in the fields so he was on his own in a block of three— with Drum in the middle stable. The nameplates on either side of the two stable doors declared that they were the unoccupied homes of BAMBI and MOTH. The three stables opposite had the nameplates BLUEY, TIFFANY, and DOLLY DAYDREAM on their bottom doors, and farther stables around the corner were the homes of MR. HIGGINS, LESTER, PIPPIN, and HENRY, apparently. All empty. No wonder my pony was irritated—this was to be his new home and I could tell he was far from impressed!

"Sorry, babe!" I whispered to him. "The only other yard I liked was *way* too expensive and this one is close enough to bike to."

I put Drum's tack on the spare saddle rack and bridle hook in the tack room before transferring all his other belongings from Mom's car to the barn where everyone had their place for feed, cleaning-out tools, rugs, and grooming kits. Then I mixed Drummer's evening feed.

He's just over fourteen hands, *the* most gorgeous bright bay, without a single white marking anywhere. Totally bay is Drum! Seeing me arrive with the bucket cheered him up a bit and then, after checking his hay net and water bucket and kissing his nose, I kicked the bottom bolt shut on his stable and walked to Mom's car. I didn't dare look back because I knew Drummer would be looking after me accusingly, his eyes saying, "You're not leaving me *here,* are you?"

"How's our boy doing?" asked Mom, twiddling with the car radio. She had followed the horse trailer we'd hired to transport Drummer to his new home and had been sitting inside while I settled Drum, the noise of music from the CD player and radio muffled by the sound of raindrops.

"He's OK. Although he probably thinks he's been sold," I added, glumly. I didn't mention the rat. I've discovered it is best not to worry parents with the everyday comings and goings of wildlife at a stable yard. They never understand and start muttering hysterically about rabies and the like. I felt depressed enough already.

I spent the evening sticking up Drummer's photographs and award ribbons in my new (teeny-weeny) bedroom (which has flowery wallpaper—disgusting—and I can't wait to paint it. I'd *love* dark purple walls, but Mom's really against it and says the room's too small. She'd got a point because our new house is a two rooms upstairs and two rooms downstairs style cottage. Tiny. So Mom has said no to purple walls. I think she's scared I'll turn into a Goth. No chance—I can't wear a bunch of piercings with a riding hat; I'd look totally odd. Anyway, with all she's been through lately with Dad running off with Skinny Lynny (or at least that's what I called her), I didn't want to upset her. I'll have purple walls later on when she's more like Mom, if that ever happens).

With tomorrow being Saturday, I planned to cycle to the yard early and get to know the locals. Me and Drum had such a great time with our friends at our last yard. There was a whole gang of us, and when we weren't riding, we were always hanging around and enjoying just being with our ponies. Remembering how it had been made me homesick. I don't miss our old house, but I really miss my old riding friends. I bet poor Drummer's homesick as well. After all, he's left his old pals, too. And it's all Lyn's fault. And Dad's.

Anyway, once the ribbons and pictures were on the walls, my room looked a bit better, even with the old lady decor, and I went down for dinner with Mom. She's been better since we bought this house—she was really sad until we moved out of the house we'd lived in with Dad. We were both stunned when he said he'd found someone else (he said he hadn't meant to, he didn't want to hurt us, Lyn was his *soul mate*, blah blah, yak yak, yeah yeah). I couldn't understand it, I mean, he and Mom are *married*. They're my *parents*. How come he can leave both of us for that…that… well, Mom and I think Dad's so-called soul mate might have an eating disorder (I almost hope so). And she wears designer clothes and has superstraight hair. Which is streaked. She's not all bubbly and funny like Mom (or how Mom used to be before the soul mate stole Dad away); Lyn's just all snotty and cold. Whenever I've seen her, she's just looked bored. I hate her. She's a witch and she's cast a spell on my dad. I just can't understand what he sees in her. It's not like she's drop-dead gorgeous, just thin and pale with a face as long as Drum's tail. Yuck.

Mom's not like Skinny Lynny. She's in her early thirties and she used to be a bit chubby—although she's lost lots of weight lately, stress, I guess. She mainly wears jeans and a T-shirt and her hair is sort of wavy and just one color—kind of darkish blond. I've got reddish brown hair like Drummer's coat—oh, and my dad. When Dad first moved out of our last house, Mom said he was having an early midlife crisis and he'd be back, but he didn't come back and we had to move here. Before we did I heard Mom talking on the phone to her (nightmare, I'll fill you in later) friend Carol from work, saying that when we moved she was going to have a makeover, like those sad women on TV. Not surgery, we can't afford it, but hair and makeup and stuff. Scary!

Dad pays for Drummer. It's a guilt trip, naturally, but I don't know what I'd do without Drum so I'm relieved he's still putting up the cash for his livery. And after all, he is my dad; I do love him and all that. I feel sorry for Mom, though. I used to hear crying at night when it first happened. Still, like I said, she seems a little better since we moved here.

"Oh, Pia, remember I need you to show me how to work your new computer," Mom said between mouthfuls of her dinner. At least she was eating again; she ate practically nothing when Dad first moved out.

"What for?" I asked. We got a new computer for my homework; the old one was on its last legs and kept going down. I'd be in the middle of researching something and suddenly *ping*, black screen, whiny downward noise. I mean, *ahhh!*

"I want to go on the Internet," she replied. So after dinner I showed her all the differences in our new Apple Mac—not at all like the PC Mom uses for work. She works—mainly from home—for a marketing company on a project for a top car manufacturer, helping to run their company car drivers' club. She was still Googling when I went to bed. I hope she doesn't get hooked on eBay. My friend Kirsten's mom started buying stuff from there and it wasn't long before they couldn't move in their house for other people's trash cluttering up the place. I shouldn't have thought about Kirsten; I felt even more homesick. Texting her from under the sheets, I told her about the hot boy. That'll get her going!

Saturday was sunny and when I arrived at the yard, it looked very different to how it had the night before. Under the deluge I hadn't noticed the flowers in tubs, and everywhere it looked much cleaner—no sign of Mister Rat. There was even a pretty dappled gray pony looking out over the DOLLY DAYDREAM nameplate opposite Drum. Drummer neighed when he saw me—he probably wondered whether I was ever coming back—and I went in and reassured him, giving him a couple of carrots that he chomped greedily. As I struggled to untie his hay net (Drum twists it around and around in the night so I have this struggle every morning), I heard hoofbeats and voices outside. We were not alone.

"I'm moving Bambi next door today," said a voice.

"You sneaky thing, I bet you haven't asked Mrs. C either," someone else replied.

"It's right next door! That batty old woman won't even notice once I've moved my nameplate," the first voice said as the hoofbeats got louder and closer.

"I bet it won't make any difference; you still won't get a date with you-know-who," the second voice giggled.

"We'll see," said the first voice.

Then, the nerve of it, someone opened Drum's stable door. Luckily, I was quick enough to grab his forelock, or else he could have been out loose on the yard, an idea I wasn't very pleased with.

"Er, can I help you?" I asked. A girl about my own age with short, dark brown hair looked at me incredulously with deep green eyes. She was pretty, with small, elfin features, and she wore a red T-shirt and a rather grubby pair of pale blue jodhpurs. Clearly, I was a surprise.

7

"What are you doing in here?" she asked, rather rudely. She held a skewbald mare at the end of a lead rope. Her brown patches were bright chestnut, her mane and tail were white, and her fine chestnut-colored head was divided by a wide, white blaze running from between her eyes to her nostrils. Drum, pleased to see another pony at last, strained over my shoulder to say hello. The skewbald's ears jammed back along her neck and she squealed and stamped a front hoof indignantly. She wasn't at all pleased to see Drum— talk about overreacting! Pushing him back, I grabbed the door and closed it again.

"Mrs. Collins said I would get this stable for my pony Drummer," I explained. From the look on the girl's face, this was not welcome news.

"Well, I'm sorry to disappoint you, but I'm moving in here today. You'll have to get out—you can have my old stable; it's only next door," she said.

Do you know what? If the girl had asked me nicely, I would have been happy to swap stables; it meant nothing to me, but something just got me about the way the girl *expected* me to move. She hadn't asked me; she had *told* me. Behind her, I could see the other girl, who looked older and a good deal tidier, holding a good-looking brownish-gray pony encased in a turnout rug, despite it being summer. She looked like she expected me to move, too. How easy it would have been to say OK, but I didn't. Instead, I felt the hair on the back of my neck rising like a Jack Russell. Who did she think she was, bossing me around?

8

The girl pressed her lips together and jutted out her chin, daring me to argue with her. So I did. I hadn't wanted to move away from my friends—I'd been made to, I hadn't wanted to move Drum here—that had been forced upon me, too, and I hadn't wanted my dad to run off with some skinny woman from work, which had started it all. I was fed up with being told what to do, and something snapped. No more—this was the end.

"I'm not going anywhere," I heard myself say (quite aggressively, actually, I kind of surprised myself). "Mrs. Collins made it clear I was to have this stable, so Drummer stays put."

The girl didn't take this at all well. But, then, come on, she'd started it. She hadn't finished either.

"You've got a lot of nerve for a new girl," she said. "It can't matter to you which stable you're in, and there's nothing wrong with Bambi's old stable. Come on, you can easily move; it won't take a minute."

I could. But I wasn't going to. My blood was up and the girl standing in front of me suddenly represented everyone who had made me do things I hadn't wanted to do. I wasn't budging.

"I'm sorry," I said in a tone that sounded anything but. "It would unsettle Drummer to move again. He's staying in this stable."

"You're a sneaky one," said the girl, narrowing her eyes at me. "Like your chances, do you?" And with that, she turned around and led who I presumed was Bambi into the stable next door, slamming the door shut behind her. The girl with the brownish-gray pony raised her eyebrows at me before taking off to another part of the yard.

I felt churned up and a bit fluttery—you know what it's like. What on earth had just happened? What did the girl mean by asking whether I liked my chances? For one horrible moment I had thought she was going to start a fight—thank goodness she hadn't. I'd only been there about eighteen hours and things were not going well. I should have just moved out when she asked, but then I remembered she hadn't asked. I would have hated myself if I'd meekly given in to the girl next door. And so I didn't hate myself—but the girl next door did. Great. Nice going, Pia, good job, I congratulated myself on making an enemy on my first day.

And things didn't get any better as the morning wore on. When I went to grab my grooming kit, Drum decided he loved Bambi. Bambi decided she hated Drum. I came back to see Drum reaching over his door to talk to Bambi and the skewbald stamping and squealing like her honor was at stake. The skewbald's owner did not see the funny side. Hardly a surprise, I thought.

"Can you keep your nosy pony under control?" she asked. As if!

"He's only being friendly," I said defensively.

"Your pony's being a huge pain and Bambi's going nuts." Bambi was, indeed, going nuts. Drum just stretched toward her even more—he obviously thought she was playing hard to get. I felt myself getting irritated; after all,

Drum was being nice, while it was frosty old Bambi who was being a pain. I'd heard it said that owners and their animals were alike; those two couldn't be more like peas in a pod if they tried. What a whiny brat! She obviously didn't care that Drum was lonely, and he was being really nice to the horrible Bambi. I didn't know what to say, but just then, the brownish-gray pony returned, ridden by the girl who—and I hadn't noticed before—had about a zillion earrings all along one ear (so I was wrong; obviously you can have multiple piercings under a riding hat because she was living proof).

"Are you coming, Cat, or not?" she asked.

"You bet," replied the girl, throwing a saddle on her pony's back. "I can't wait to get away from Bambi's pesky new neighbor," she added rudely.

Cat eventually tacked up and the pair rode out of the yard without a backward glance. I could hear Cat moaning to her friend about new people and ponies and how they upset everyone, like I couldn't hear her, and I felt really upset. They didn't even know me! How unfair. I imagined a pitchfork accidentally falling on Cat (what sort of name is that, anyway? Apt, though, *mee-ow!*) and felt a little better.

Drum nudged me for an apple. "Where's my treat, Mom?" he seemed to say. I told him he hadn't helped, giving Bambi the eye, and he just looked at me blankly, so I tied him up outside his stable and got down to some serious cleaning out. I'd almost finished when I heard hoofbeats again and hoped it wasn't horrible Cat back.

It wasn't. It was a girl with red hair and about a million freckles on a blue roan and a girl with a long blond braid on a palomino. Jumping off, they put their ponies into two opposite empty stables, next to the dappled gray. I didn't know whether to say anything or not—my experience with Cat had put me off being friendly. Anyway, I thought, I'm the new girl; it's up to them to make me feel welcome, surely? I was still dithering when the girl with the red hair put her freckled face over the door.

"Hi!" she said. "I'm Katy. Who are you?"

"Hi, I'm Pia," I replied. Thank goodness, I thought, someone normal!

"How come you've got this stable, then?" asked Katy. *Ding ding ding*, warning bells, not so normal, after all. What was it about this stable? Buried treasure under the floor? Entrance to the magical kingdom?

"Mrs. Collins said I was to have this stable," I said firmly. "This is Drummer, by the way," I said, trying to get onto safer ground.

"Oh, only I know Cat wanted this stable. She kept on about it as soon as Shelly left. I thought she'd be in here. Not you. Hello, Drummer," she added, patting Drum's nose.

"What's so special about this stable?" I asked. It looked exactly like Bambi's stable to me. No bigger, no better.

"Oh, nothing, nothing at all," said Katy, hastily, "except that…well, I bet Cat makes Mrs. Collins give it to her, so I wouldn't get too comfortable if I were you."

"I've already told her she can't have it," I said.

"*Oooh*, what did she say?" asked Katy, her eyes wide with awe.

"Not much," I lied.

"Well, good luck with that!" said Katy, in a way that suggested that mere luck wouldn't be enough. "Gotta go!" she added, running off again.

"We'd better get your nameplate on the door ASAP, shouldn't we?" I said to Drummer. I felt determined that Cat wasn't going to have her own way about the stable. Why should she? I pushed the wheelbarrow around to the muck heap. Katy and her friend were sitting in the sun eating chips, and when they saw me, it suddenly went very quiet, a sure sign they'd been talking about *me*. I felt my stomach lurch. It was like being the new girl at school (that reminds me, I've got that to look forward to!). I thought I'd make an effort so I smiled and they smiled back. Well, I say smile. You know the sort of smile where someone's mouth does all the right things, but their eyes look like they really, *really* hate you? Fake smiles. I decided they were weirdos—the entire bunch of them! I had to go riding before I went crazy. As I tacked up I informed Drummer that we'd come to a stable yard full of freaks—I thought he ought to know, in case the ponies were the same. He looked at me sideways. "Told you it was a dump," he seemed to say. Jamming on my hat, I led Drum into the yard and swung myself into his saddle.

"I don't know where we're going, Drum, but I'm not going to ask anyone here whether we can go riding

with them. Besides, how lost can we get?" I said, trying
to sound upbeat. Drummer shook his mane and sneezed
and we headed out on the bridle way through the woods.
It seemed to be us against the world. Well, bring it on, I
thought, angrily, I can deal with it!

CHAPTER 2

ONCE IN THE SADDLE, I felt a bit better. Drummer would make new friends, and there were bound to be people at the yard who were nice—Katy seemed normal. I just had to bide my time and win them over. I tried not to think about our old friends back home. Kirsten had replied to my text and told me how she and the gang were going to our local show next weekend. Then I remembered that it was *her* local show, but it wasn't mine anymore. I felt a sickening lurch—Drum and I had won the Handy Pony class last year. I wished with all my heart we'd never had to leave home. Home. I didn't think we would ever be able to call this our home. For one dreadful moment, I thought I was going to cry, but I gulped back the tears, concentrating very hard on Drummer's red ears bobbing along in front of me. They're great ears; they have black tips and point inward at the top because Drum is part Arab.

The woods were cool and the sun shone through in shafts like spotlights. After yesterday's rain, steam rose from the ground and Drummer's black hooves made solid prints in the mud. I'm not supposed to go riding in strange places alone, but I was hardly going to wait for someone at the yard to show me around. Forget that! They'd think I was a baby if I asked them. I had my cell phone in my pocket and I was sure we'd be fine. Besides, if we followed the tracks, it made sense that we wouldn't get lost.

Drummer felt a bit fresh—we were in new surroundings and he'd spent last night in his stable instead of turned out in the field as usual. Drum is no plodder, and he can put in an impressive buck when he wants to. I stroked his mane and told him to be good.

"We have to look after each other, Drum," I told him. I didn't add that we only had each other, and everyone else seemed to hate us. He just snorted—which wasn't a good sign because he does that when he's on his toes, so I shoved my heels down and my knees in and decided I'd better keep my wits about me. At least it took my mind off sobbing like a baby. Why hadn't I just moved into Bambi's stable? No problem, no worries, no enemy. How stupid was I?

The woods opened up onto a field and we followed hoofprints around the outside track. Pushing Drummer into a trot, I was just hoping we wouldn't come across Cat and her rude friend on the brownish-gray pony when Drummer gave another snort. Oh, dear. I felt his back go up under the saddle—yep, he was *dying* to buck.

"Behave!" I told him, sharply, and kept him at trot—it's more difficult for him to buck in trot—but he shook his head, still threatening to do a handstand. I could tell he thought it was funny. Don't you just love a pony with a sense of humor? We trotted for ages because I wanted to get the tickle out of his toes and then, when we got to some more woods, I slowed him down to a walk, patting his neck and telling him how good he was, hoping he'd take the hint. He seemed more settled. When we reached another stretch of grass, I was feeling so miserable again I decided to chance it and pushed him into canter. It was great—I could hear the birds singing, the wind rustling through the leaves in the trees, and Drummer's hoofbeats on the grass, and then, suddenly, I was flying through the air and landing on the ground.

Splat!

I'm going to *kill* Drummer! was my first thought, anger taking over from my self-pity. This was immediately followed by the realization that no one would bother looking for me and if I was injured I could lie in the wet grass for hours. I then felt that sinking feeling, knowing that Mom was going to be furious when she found out we'd been out alone.

Then I realized that I wasn't hurt and that it would be better to get up and catch my pony so that I could carry out my first thought and not worry about the others. But Drum was on the ground, too. He hadn't bucked me off but had stumbled and fallen. Poor Drummer! Jumping up and shelving any thoughts I had of doing him in, I grabbed his reins as he scrambled to his feet. He looked surprised and offended! "How did I end up here?" his face said.

"Steady, boy, it's all right, just stand," I whispered, stroking his neck and checking his legs for injuries. Walking around he seemed OK, just bewildered. Then I realized my elbow hurt, but it wasn't broken or anything, and we were both covered in mud down one side.

Embarrassing, but not life threatening. I decided I'd worry about that later. I hadn't thought I could feel any more humiliated this morning, but clearly I'd been wrong. The whole morning was turning into a pile of poo.

Then I caught sight of something in the grass and I bent down to pick it up. It was small and dark, made of some sort of stone, and looked old and weathered. It was a tiny statue of a person on a horse, less than two inches long. I held it in my hand and wondered whether Drum had stumbled on it, whether it was responsible for our fall. The person was sitting sidesaddle, so it had to be a woman. Her features were indistinguishable, although her nose was missing and the horse had only one ear.

"As if today wasn't bad enough," I heard someone say. I looked up sharply, but there was no one there.

"Now I've got mud in my ear." Still no one there, just Drummer rubbing his head against his leg. I wondered whether I had a concussion, but I knew I hadn't lost consciousness, which is how you can tell.

"Moving stables, diva next-door neighbor, and now this. Today stinks." I looked down at the statue in my hand. It couldn't be that talking, but the only alternative was too fantastic to even think about. I really couldn't go there.

"And she's more bothered about her new treasure than me," said the voice. "I want to go home. And I don't mean that *dump* we've just come from!"

"Drummer?" I looked at him. He looked sharply back at me.

"Oh, what? What now?" said the voice.

"Have you got mud in your ear?" I looked around again, this time to see whether anyone could see me talking to my pony. I mean, I talk to him all the time, but I never expect him to talk back. I mean, who would imagine they could have a conversation with their pony?

"Oh, no," groaned Drummer, dramatically, "don't say you can hear me. As if I haven't got enough to worry about!"

"I've got a lot to worry about, too, you know," I told him. Drum blinked. Twice.

"Can you really hear me?" he asked.

"Yes," I said, feeling very weird. "You just said you've got a diva next-door neighbor and today stinks."

Drummer gulped. "Nah, can't be happening. It must be something I ate. Something weird at that new yard. Humans can't hear me. *You* can't hear me. Just so not happening!"

"Well, I can hear you! What's with all that?"

"Well, she *is* a diva, and today does..."

"No, I mean, me being able to hear you!"

"How should I know?" said my pony. My knees felt a bit wobbly and gave way and I sat on the ground, letting the statue fall. The grass was wet. Yuck. I got back up again and tottered about a bit like a newborn foal.

"How come you can speak all of a sudden?" I asked. Silence. Drummer stood mute as before, looking at me. Taking off my riding hat, I ran my fingers through my hair. First my pony talked to me, and then he didn't. Was I going crazy? Yes, that was it, I was going crazy.

Well, I thought, that's all right then, that clears that up! I'm bonkers. But at least my pony had stopped talking. That was something. I bent down and picked up the statue.

"...so can you hear me or not? Make up your mind," said the same voice as before. Drummer's voice.

"Yes, yes, I can hear you. Why did you stop speaking?" I asked him. I was talking to my pony like it was the most normal thing in the world.

"I didn't. I'm always telling you things, but you can't hear me. At least, you couldn't until a minute ago," he replied. I looked again at the statue.

A figure on a horse...

"Keep talking," I said.

"What do you want me to say?" said Drum.

"It doesn't matter, but don't stop," I said.

"OK, I can tell you how I feel about being dragged to a new stable yard with ponies I don't know, and a good-looking neighbor with a very bad-looking personality..."

I put the statue on the ground and Drum went silent as soon as it left my hand. So I picked it up once more and immediately heard Drum again, "...but the gray looks quite nice, she's been giving me the eye and—"

"Drummer," I interrupted, "it's this thing. This is the *catalyst*. When I hold this figure, I can hear you, but when I put it down, I can't."

"Oh," said Drum, sniffing the statue. "What do you think it is, then? Magic?"

"It must be. But what exactly it is, or what it represents, I have no idea."

"Well, you'd better not leave it here," said my pony. "That stuck-up Cat might find it and I don't want a cozy little chat with *her*. Let's go, I'd like another canter, if you're up for it, and then we can go home. I mean real home, not that horrible place we've just come from."

"No bucking, though, or else!" I threatened, ignoring what he'd said about home before I welled up again. Drum just snorted. He knows I'd never do anything to hurt him, not really. Mounting again, I put the statue in the pocket of my waistcoat, zipping it up to make sure it didn't fall out. It was some find! It was worth a dirty pony and a sore elbow if it meant I could hear what my pony was saying. Wow, the day was picking up! Even with the statue in my pocket I could hear Drum mumbling to himself.

We found our way around the bridle paths and woods—Drum could tell where the yard was, so there was no danger of us getting lost—although he refused to tell me exactly how he could tell. "It's just my superior equine sense of direction," is all I got out of him. And when we arrived back at the yard, the hateful Cat was still there, getting ready to turn out her skewbald. There was no chance she hadn't noticed the mud on us. I thought she might have said something, but she ignored us as she led Bambi out to the field. As I put Drum in his stable, I heard another voice.

"Hi, good-looking. You're back then. Taken a tumble?"

I turned around expecting to see Cat back, but the yard was empty. Drum whispered to me, "Uh-oh, it's the dappled gray opposite, the one in the Dolly Daydream stable. I told you she had her eye on me."

"Do you mean she likes you?" I asked.

"Well, see what you think."

"Coming out in the field tonight?" asked the gray. She sounded very keen. Drummer looked at me. I shook my head. "Not yet. Better give it another night in."

My pony looked relieved. "Apparently not," he explained to his admirer.

"Oh, well," she replied, "I expect you will soon, and I'm not going anywhere."

I put Drummer's bed down—forking the straw into a deep layer with big banks up the sides. It looked very cozy. When I came back from putting the tools away, Drum had dug it all up and was rolling in it. The whole stable looked like a complete mess.

"Hey!" I hissed. "I've just made that bed, you ungrateful pony." It was something I'd said a hundred times before, only this time, my comments didn't go unanswered.

"It's my bed, and I like it like this. You do what you want to your bed," said Drummer, rolling again before getting to his feet and shaking off the straw. He wasn't very successful—bits of straw clung to his mane and tail so I had to get a brush and tidy him up as well as redo the bed.

With Drummer looking respectable, his water bucket filled, and his hay net hung, I gave him a kiss on the nose

(*"Yuck!"* he said, very rudely) and told him I'd see him later to redo his bed and hay net. Then I heard the gray again and what she said made a shiver go up and down my spine.

"Oh, dear, my stomach hurts. Ow! It really, really hurts."

Now stomachache in horses is serious. It means colic and, because horses and ponies can't be sick, if there is anything wrong or anything blocks the intestine, the horse can get so ill it can die. Anyone horsey knows how bad colic can be, and how it can be a matter of life and death, so this was something I couldn't ignore—however much I wanted to. So, feeling very strange and hoping no one could see me, I walked over to the gray's stable and, glancing around one last time and feeling rather foolish, asked her whether I had heard her correctly, and did she have a stomachache.

"Yes," said the gray. Then her head jerked up and she narrowed her eyes. "How come you can hear me?"

"She just can, take it from me," Drummer called from the other side of the yard between mouthfuls of hay. The gray looked less suspicious. Her eyes softened and she hung her head—she looked in pain.

"I feel awful. Can you help me?"

"Where's your owner?" I asked.

"Dee-Dee's in the barn, I think. Ouch, there's another pang. Oooh, it really hurts and I want to go to the bathroom, but I can't seem to."

"I'll get her to call the vet," I said.

"Oh, no, not the vet!" The gray's eyes widened.

"They can't wait to put their hands in places hands were never meant to go. I feel better now…honest…ouch, maybe not."

I made my way to the barn. I had to tell the gray's owner about the pony's condition, but I hadn't figured out how to explain how I knew. When I got to the barn, there were three girls in there: Cat (oh, hooray!), the blond girl I had seen on the palomino, and another girl with long brown hair whom I'd seen with the gray earlier.

"Are you Dolly Daydream's owner?" I asked. My heart was thumping in my chest, but I knew I had to face this. The girl nodded. Cat ignored me as though I were a bale of hay.

"Er, erm, I think she's got colic," I said.

"What? She was all right a moment ago," said the girl.

"How do you know?" asked Cat. I didn't think they'd believe me if I told them. "Well, Dolly told me herself," didn't sound like a very clever thing to say, so I just shrugged my shoulders. "She really has," I said. "Honestly."

Pushing past me, the girl ran to her pony's stable and looked over the door. Cat and the blond girl followed her and I trailed behind. When we all got there, the girl turned round and stared at me.

"What are you talking about?" she said. I glanced at the gray. She looked perfectly healthy and I wondered whether I was still bonkers, or the gray had been having a laugh at my expense. She seemed fine.

"She's fine," said the girl. OK, OK, no need to rub it in. I wished I'd minded my own business, but Drummer shouted across from the stable and nobody heard him but me.

"She's not fine; she feels awful and in an hour or so she'll be rolling around and covered in sweat. Tell her to call the vet."

"You need to call the vet," I heard myself saying. Why was I doing this? There had to be a better way to get *everyone* to hate me.

"Are you sick or something?" said Cat. "You're the one who needs medical attention. Dolly's fine. Why are you scaring Dee?"

"Who are you, anyway?" asked Dolly's owner—Dee, I presumed.

"She's the one in Shelly's old stable. The one whose pony keeps harassing Bambi," snarled Cat.

"Drum does not *harass* Bambi; he just likes her, that's all," I heard myself saying, making things worse.

"You tell 'em," Drummer heckled from his stable. It was good to have some moral support, even if no one but me heard it.

"Well, I think you should mind your own business, thank you," said Dee, and we all went to turn away when Dolly let out a groan that everyone heard and started pawing the ground. Dashing back, we all leaned over the stable door. There was Dolly, showing the classic signs of colic, pawing the ground and looking around at her flanks. Sweat had broken out on her neck and she groaned again.

"Oh, my God," said Dee, pulling out her cell and scrolling through numbers. "Where's the vet's number, for goodness' sake?"

It all got a little confusing after that.

CHAPTER 3

WHEN I GOT TO the stables the next day, I was relieved to see Dolly munching on her hay as though nothing had happened. Actually, quite a lot had happened: Dee's mom (who is the sort of blond woman who manages to look glamorous in riding clothes) had arrived in a state of near hysteria, wailing about a big show Dolly was entered for (apparently, Dee and Dolly go showing, and from what I could gather, it's more for her mom's benefit than Dee's—even though Dee's mom has her own horse, Lester, at the yard, too).

Anyway, they had a bit of a shouting match, which only ended when the vet cleared his throat and asked whether anyone cared about the patient, which was what he was there for, after all, and this resulted in embarrassed faces all around. The vet went on to say it was lucky Dolly's colic had been caught early and because of this Dolly had got better, not worse. Dee had burst into tears at least three times and kept thanking me for noticing Dolly's condition. She kept saying Dolly might have died—but luckily, Dolly was alive and well this morning. Whew.

Dee's mom had kept on saying thank goodness somebody bothered about the expensive pony she'd bought for her ungrateful daughter, and what a pity Dee hadn't noticed, which was hardly fair. I mean, Dolly had *told* me she was ill; I could hardly take any credit for just hearing her—but I didn't dare say anything. No point demonstrating just what a complete lunatic they had on the yard. No way! So I just sort of chewed my lip and smiled a bit and tried not to take any credit, even though Dee's mom kept thanking me.

So that was the excitement of yesterday evening, and this was now. Petting Squish the greyhound, I made my way to Drum's stable. My dear pony's greeting was nothing short of splendid.

"Oh, you've decided to turn up at last, so perhaps now I can have my breakfast. Time to get moving!" As I still had our little stone sidesaddle friend we'd found yesterday in my pocket, I heard every word.

"Nice to see you, too. Don't you think that's kind of rude?" Drum looked at me and gulped.

"Oh," he said, "you can still hear me, then? I was hoping that was just a one-time-only event. Anyway, as you *can* hear me, how about getting me my breakfast? You might as well make yourself useful."

I looked at him and shook my head. "I'd always imagined you to be a polite pony," I told him. For an answer, Drummer just lifted his tail and pooped in his bed. Charming!

Dee-Dee was in the barn and she actually said hello to me and was quite friendly, asking me about Drum and telling me that Dolly was much better this morning, though, of course, they'd had to miss the show.

"I wouldn't have wished Dolly to have colic, but I'm glad we don't have to spend all day running around in circles surrounded by all the other overcompetitive moms," she said.

"I love taking Drummer to shows," I told her, "but, of course, we don't do it very seriously."

"It's all right for you. My mom takes it very seriously," said Dee. "If we come back with a yellow ribbon, it's been a bad day. Red and blue are OK, but anything else means a postmortem analysis in the car on the way home and booking a lesson with one of the top show producers. Another Saturday is down the drain," she moaned.

Thanking my lucky stars my mom wasn't like that, and realizing the big, fancy horse trailer parked up by the outdoor school belonged to Dee's mom, I grabbed Drum's breakfast and the cleaning-out tools so I could clean his stable while he demolished his feed tied up on the yard outside.

"There's practically *nothing* here," Drum complained, licking the bucket dramatically.

"We're riding, and you can't do that on a full stomach," I told him. "That handful of pony nuts is just a token gesture."

"Then you won't mind if I reciprocate with a gesture of my own, token or otherwise," Drum replied, lifting his tail and pooping on the yard.

I gave him a look. For one, I didn't realize ponies knew words like *reciprocate*, and two, how rude was that?

"You've just done one of those in your stable!" I exclaimed.

"Plenty more where that came from," said Drummer, licking his lips.

I cleaned up with a broom and shovel.

"You're right about one thing," I said, throwing the tools in the wheelbarrow. "I do seem to be your slave."

"Not when you consider that *you're* the one doing the riding, and I'm the one doing all the work!" Drummer replied. "You missed a bit…" he added.

I had decided to do some schooling in the outdoor school this morning. Once I had groomed and tacked up (and Drum had pulled a face and told me at length how he considered schooling to be *the most utterly boring thing ever*), we let ourselves into the outdoor school. Good, no one around. I didn't know where Dee had gone, but she wasn't likely to join us with Dolly having just had colic. After warming up (with Drum yawning dramatically, just to rub it in), I told him I wanted to concentrate on our lateral work—moving sideways. I was quite excited—being able to communicate with Drum could really help us with our schooling. I saw us taking the horse ballet world by storm. Awards and trophies would be ours. I'd be famous—how cool! I might even make the *Horsey Press*. I'd always fancied myself being interviewed and being on TV. I could *so* be the next big name in horse ballet. A horsey celebrity. Oh, yes, I could quite see me in the role. Drum seemed less than excited.

"Schooling's *so* boring. Let's go for a ride, instead. I promise I won't buck," he added.

"Oh, Drum, come on," I pleaded. "When I put my leg back here behind the girth, you're supposed to go sideways. Just try."

"The trouble is," said Drum, sounding very superior, "you don't put your body in the right place. I would go to the left, but your body weight is tipped to the right. It unbalances me. Fix yourself and I'll do it fine!"

I was just thinking about this when I heard the click of the gate. Bad news! It was Bambi and Cat, and the palomino that lived next to Dolly, ridden by the girl with very long blond hair. The hair was tied back with a bright red ribbon and the girl wore a matching red sweater and black jodhpurs. Cat wore green jodhpurs, a pale blue sweatshirt, and a purple skullcap cover on her hat. With Bambi's brown and white patched coat, they looked like they were going for a circus audition.

I swore under my breath. Just who I *didn't* want to see.

"Perhaps you'd like to go riding, *now?*" Drum asked in a smug voice.

"No, definitely not," I replied. "We're not being driven out by anyone. Now be quiet."

"Why? They can't hear *me*—but they can hear *you*. You're the one who needs to shut up!"

Drum was right. If they heard me, they'd think I was a complete freak. We went back to our schooling and I concentrated on getting my body weight right. It seemed to work—sort of. The blond girl managed a half smile in my direction and rode in the other half of the outdoor school, but it seemed that Cat kept deliberately riding in my way. And, of course, bad-tempered Bambi pulled faces at Drum whenever they passed us.

"She's a bit feisty," exclaimed Drum with a snort. "I like them like that!"

"Why can't you like Dolly?" I hissed. "She likes you."

"She's scary."

"And Bambi isn't?"

"She'll come around!"

I was at the point of thinking it might be OK to go for a ride without seeming to have been frightened off by the company when the gate clicked again and my heart did a sort of flip. It was the hot boy on his chestnut pony. There was no way I was going now!

We rode around. I tried to do all the things I was good at so I wouldn't look stupid. Cat had turned into sweetness and light upon the boy's arrival. Typical! Then she and her blond friend went into another conference in the middle of the school. I'd noticed the palomino pony nodding her head up and down. As we rode past I couldn't hear what Cat and her friend were saying, but I could hear the ponies.

"I wish she'd take this *off!*" said the palomino.

"Can't you just ignore it?" asked Bambi. "I ignore mine."

"I can't. I keep getting flashbacks to when..."

Drum and I rode out of earshot at this point. I was so intrigued, I did a ten-yard circle so I could ride past them again.

"You'd think Bean would catch on. I mean, you've been shaking your head for ages now," said Bambi, between face-pulling at Drum.

"Well, that's just what I thought. But all she does is get my ears and my teeth checked. Honestly! Humans are so slow!"

"It's a shame it's so tight," said Bambi.

"It's a shame it's on at all," replied the palomino, shaking her head again.

"Oh, here's that pesky new bay again, giving me the eye. Get lost!" Bambi hissed to Drum.

"Can't *you* just ignore *him?*" asked the palomino. "I think he's rather cute."

We rode out of earshot again.

"Hear that?" asked Drummer in a smug voice. "All the fillies love the Drummer!"

"Except Bambi!" I replied. Unfortunately, the boy rode past us as I said it and gave me a strange look. Great, I thought. Good start, Pia, nicely done. I congratulated myself on being a complete dingbat. Then I started thinking about the palomino pony. What was too tight? I looked at her bridle. She wore a bog-standard bridle with a flash noseband that crossed over her nose. Sometimes they can be fastened a bit tight and not all ponies like them, but this one didn't look especially snug and it was well fitted. What was making the palomino shake her head?

As we rode past the next time, the blond girl said, "It must be the pollen. Head shakers are supposed to hate pollen."

"But she started it in the winter," said Cat.

"Mmmm, global warming?" suggested the blond girl.

"You've had her teeth checked like I suggested, and..." said Cat. I rode out of earshot. I was dying to follow to hear some more but didn't dare. Then the boy joined them. He'd been storming around on his chestnut cob with a

33

wide white blaze and four white stockings—she had cantered with her nose on her chest, white feather on her legs flying, snorting at every stride, like a medieval charger up for a joust. The boy didn't seem at all worried; he just sat there with his stirrups two holes too long, his back dead straight, used to her, the fringes on the striped Indian blanket under the saddle flapping as the chestnut bobbed along. But now they were with the others and as I rode past again I heard more tantalizing conversation.

"You've checked the fit of her bridle?" asked the boy.

"Yes!" said the blond girl.

"It's the noseband," I heard the palomino say. "Take it off me!"

"If they only knew about your injury when you were younger…" said Bambi.

This was too much. I had to stop and listen. I put Drum into a square halt and pretended to practice our rein-back. It's our worst movement so we looked very amateurish, but it couldn't be helped.

"That rope around my nose, it just got tighter and tighter. I can't bear anything tight around it now. The plain old noseband was OK, but this new one is *so* annoying!"

"You didn't mind it at first," said Bambi.

"I know, but then I got all sweaty one day, the leather got all stiff, and even though it's soft now, I can't get past it. It just takes me right back to when I was injured, and I can't stand it!"

I looked across at the palomino. She looked so miserable.

Come to that, so did her rider. It couldn't be much fun riding a pony that did nothing but shake its head.

Drum stuck his oar in. "Why don't you say something?" he hissed. "I'm sure you'd impress wonder boy. Go on, get in there!"

The thought had occurred to me, although, of course, I wanted to help the palomino; that was a given.

"Excuse me," I said, "but I couldn't help overhearing your conversation. About your pony's head shaking," They all looked at me blankly. "Have you tried taking the noseband off?"

"It isn't the noseband. Tiffany had this noseband before she started shaking her head," replied the blond girl, with a look that plainly said I was suggesting the obvious.

"But you could try it?"

"It won't make any difference; it's an allergy," butted in Cat.

"She'll bolt without the noseband," the blond girl said.

"I won't, I won't, just *take it off!*" said the palomino, miserably.

"She won't bolt," I said.

"How come you know so much about what Tiffany will and won't do?" Cat snarled.

"I promise she won't run off—she really won't."

"Can you guarantee that?" said Cat. "In writing?"

"Don't be stupid, Cat," said the boy. Cat pulled a glorious face like she was sucking a lemon; she obviously didn't enjoy the boy saying that. My heart sank; I had clearly made Cat my enemy—and it had been so easy. Imagine what I could do if I really tried!

"It's an allergy," said Cat again, "and Tiffany goes well in this noseband."

"It's worth a try, though, isn't it?" said the boy. I could have kissed him. Well, to be honest, I probably could have done that without his welcome support.

"I suppose," said the blond girl, sullenly. I don't think she would have done so if the boy hadn't been there, but sliding out of the saddle, she fumbled with the straps until the noseband was in her hand and the palomino looked naked with her golden nose all exposed. The girl remounted.

"It won't make any difference," Cat said again. "And I bet she runs off," she added for good measure.

"Wow!" said the palomino pony. "How come the new girl knew that?"

"She can hear us," explained Drum.

"Get real!" said Bambi.

"I am real. She can hear what you're saying. And me and Dolly. That's how she knew Dolly was sick. Dolly told her."

"You're teasing me!" said the palomino.

"Do I look like I'm laughing?" said Drummer. "It's no bundle of laughs, believe me, I'm getting a lot of back talk."

The blond girl nudged Tiffany out onto the track and started riding around. The pony never shook her head once, just sighed. Miracle—or so it seemed to anyone who couldn't hear ponies talking.

"How did you know that?" asked the boy.

"Er…" I hadn't thought ahead far enough. Obviously, I was going to be asked questions. I thought fast. Nothing. Nada. Blank—I possessed a mind full of cobwebs with the wind whistling through it. No change there.

"Tell him you get a feeling about these things," suggested Drum.

"Well, I sort of get a feeling about these things," I heard myself mumbling. It sounded lame. Cat snorted.

"What are you then, some kind of horse whisperer?" she said, spitefully.

"Is that what you are?" asked the boy, looking at me with his blue, blue eyes. His hair, under his battered-looking hat, was blond, too—but a dark blond. Instead of jodhpurs he wore jeans and lace-up boots and a sweater with holes in it. Immediately my mind raced off on a fantasy—could he be the long-lost son of a rich banking tycoon who was switched at birth? Or a gypsy prince, whose magical way with horses no one could fathom? How old was he? What was his name?

"I'm James," he said. Whoa, not only could I talk to ponies, I was telepathic with hot boys, too. That could come in handy!

"I'm Pia," I replied, hoping my face wasn't going red.

"Pier?" interrupted Cat. "What sort of name is that?"

"What sort of name is Cat?" I replied, haughtily.

"It's short for Catriona, *actually!*"

"Oh, well, Pia isn't short for anything," I said, a little defeated.

The palomino arrived back.

"Tiffany seems to be...well...cured!" proclaimed the blond girl. "I'm Bean—my real name is Charlotte Beanie, but everyone calls me Bean."

"I'm Pia," I told her. At last someone was being normal. "And this is Drummer," I added.

"How did you know about the noseband?" asked Bean.

"She's a horse whisperer," spat out Cat, sarcastically.

"Oh, are you?" replied the blond girl, not getting Cat's mood at all. "That must be so great. How fantastic to have a horse whisperer on the yard. You'll come in very handy." She turned to Cat. "I'm going for a ride. Coming, Cat? We'll see how Tiffany is out in the open—see whether she really won't take off. I'll take the noseband, just in case." Then she turned around to me. "Would you like to come with us?" she said. Cat looked like she was going to explode.

"No," I said. "I have plans. Thanks, though."

I could see that Cat was torn between leaving me and James in the school alone together and me riding with her and Bean, but she couldn't have it both ways. As they left, I could hear Tiffany repeating to Bambi that she had no intention of bolting. I couldn't help smiling. This communication lark was so cool. I could talk to Drum and hear the other ponies. I felt for the statue in my pocket and decided I needed to find out more about it. I'd look it up on the Internet when I got home. In the meantime...

"How *did* you know about the noseband?" asked James, interrupting my thoughts. "Now Catriona's gone, you can tell me. I can see she is not a fan of yours. What have you done to upset her—except a bit of horse whispering, of course." He was teasing me. I let it go.

"I don't know why she doesn't like me," I said. "I haven't done anything to upset her—except that she wanted my stable."

"Where is your stable?"

"Next to Bambi's."

"*Ahhh*," said James softly. His next words made me go cold. "Of course, Tiffany's flash noseband was Cat's idea—Bean was having trouble stopping. Cat likes to think of herself as the yard guru and everyone asks her advice."

No wonder Cat had been pushing the noseband. Was someone up there deliberately thinking up ways I could upset Cat? Drummer interrupted my thoughts.

"Any chance of wrapping up this so-called schooling session?" he asked. "Or am I the only one getting bored stiff standing about while you chat up Romeo here?" Well, I certainly wasn't bored. Patting my oh-so-polite pony I explained to James that I should take Drummer in. We'd been there long enough. Besides, I thought, it was good to be the one to go first, play it a little cool.

I'd rubbed Drum down and put his tack away when James returned to the yard, steering his pony over to my stable and dismounting. I was flattered—see, leave them wanting more, that's the way, I told myself. Except he led his pony into the stable next to mine. His pony. Moth. My neighbor. I suddenly realized why Cat wanted Drum's stable so badly—she wanted to be next to James instead of me. No wonder she hated me, and James had realized that, too. So that's what Cat had meant about me liking my chances. She thought I liked James. OK, I might, but I hadn't even known he was my next-door neighbor then. Yikes!

I didn't feel like hanging around. Dee wandered over, and after saying hi, she leaned on Moth's half door, talking to James. I heard snatches of the story of Dolly's colic and my name was mentioned. With Drummer snug in his stable with a hay net, I got my bike and noticed James looking thoughtfully at me as I peddled toward the gate. Why was everything so complicated—I'd only been here two days, for goodness' sake!

When I got home, I fired up the computer intending to do some research on the statue so I pulled it out of my pocket and looked at it closely. A woman sitting sideways on a horse. Yes, it had to be a woman; men always used to ride astride and women sidesaddle. I wondered how old it was. Then I wondered whether it had anything to do with witchcraft, which gave me a terrifying jolt. What if I was meddling in the occult? Ah, *so* not funny!

"Are you going to be long?" Mom asked.

"Um, not sure, why?" I answered, thinking it might be time for dinner. I was hungry. Hamburgers and chips would be good. Or pasta or chili con carne...

"I want to use the computer tonight." My mom had been on the computer a lot lately. I wondered what she was doing. So I asked.

Mom went quiet. I turned round and saw her chewing her lip and going pink. Whatever *had* she been doing? My mind boggled.

"Mom?"

"Well, it was Carol's idea..." she said. My heart sank. My mom's friend Carol is a total nightmare. She's been married twice (but she's not at the moment), she has a son away at college (who only comes home to steal her money), and she always has two or three strange and pathetic boyfriends on the go. She's such a bad influence...I suddenly got a very bad feeling.

"Mom, what has Carol talked you into now?"

"Look, everyone's doing it; I thought I'd give it a try. You don't know what it's been like since your father left with Skinny. I need to have some fun, go out, meet people. It's all right for you; young people make friends so easily."

Not in my case, I thought. Little did she know.

"So what are you telling me?"

"It's just a club for single people. On the Net. Professionals. Not weirdos. Carol's been a member for years and she's met some lovely men."

"And some total lunatics!" I exclaimed. I couldn't believe my mom was Internet dating. Whatever next? Did people as old as my mom and Carol really meet people this way? Gross!

"And I'd appreciate your support," Mom continued. "I support you with your interests. The least you can do is not judge me."

I thought about it. I thought I could do that. Probably. At least I could try.

"OK, I'll try," I said. Mom looked relieved.

"Got a short list yet?" I asked.

"No. I'll keep you informed," she answered.

I wasn't sure I wanted to be kept informed. I knew too much already. Like I said, *gross!*

"Anyway," said Mom, "what are you doing on the World Wide Web?"

"Nothing," I said, switching off the computer and feeling very tired. "What's for dinner?" I asked. My statue research would have to wait. After all, there's only so much a girl can take in one day—especially when I had the ordeal of a new school lined up for the next one. I wasn't looking forward to that at all!

CHAPTER 4

YOU KNOW HOW YOU get those days where lots of things go really, really wrong, only they're mixed up with things that go really, really right so when you get to the end you can't be sure whether it was a bad day or a good one? Well, my first day at my new school was one of those days.

Guess the first person I saw when I walked into my new homeroom after an introductory chat with the principal? Yup, you've got it—the charming Catriona. Can you believe it? I give up! I spotted Cat the moment I walked through the door—her short, dark hair and her green eyes are so strikingly pretty. Worse luck. Sitting at the back of the class, she rolled her eyes in exaggerated despair as our teacher, Mrs. Stevens—wearing a tunic dress, sensible shoes, and controlled hair—introduced me to the rest of my new classmates. They stared at me in undisguised boredom; at least the ones who bothered to look up did.

"This is Pia," announced Mrs. Stevens, cheerfully, "and I know you'll all make her feel very welcome."

Total silence.

I admired Mrs. Stevens's optimism. *Welcome* was the last word I would have used to describe the reception I was getting. I saw Catriona lean over and whisper something to the girl sitting next to her and they both smirked in my direction in an anything-but-welcoming manner. My heart sank. Cat so had the advantage on me, and her confidence was obvious by the way she sprawled at her desk—all sort of diagonal and pouty. Fan-freaking-tastic!

"You can sit here, Pia, next to Toby," said Mrs. Stevens brightly, pointing to the only spare seat, next to a boy with red hair and lots of freckles.

Pulling a face, Toby leaned as far away from me as possible, like I had something nasty and contagious, which was totally unnecessary as I had no desire to cuddle up close and cozy. As I was at the front, I could feel Catriona's eyes boring into my back so I focused my thoughts on Drummer and my plans to go riding after school—I had to think of something good to get me through the day. I wished for the millionth time that my dad had never set eyes on Skinny Lynny and that I was back in my old school with all my friends, feeling like I belonged.

One change of classroom and a math class (shudder) later, the bell rang for a break and everyone trooped outside where I wandered about trying to avoid bumping into Cat, hating the feeling of being *so* out of it. This morning, Mom had gleefully waved me off with a cry of, "You'll make lots of new friends!" Grown-ups always think it's so easy to get friendly with others your own age. They seem to forget that everyone already has friends, and they don't always see the need for one more. Who wants to be seen talking with the new kid?

At lunchtime I munched my sandwiches I'd brought to avoid the misery of the cafeteria. Then I realized I had over an hour to kill before lessons started again—bored, bored, bored! But then I had a brain wave—I'd look up my little stone artifact in the library! Kirsten and I had spent cold winter lunch breaks at my old school huddled in the library. We'd sit for hours at a computer under the pretense of researching some act of parliament and then trawl famous horsey people's websites, like Alex Willard, *the* horse behaviorist who is featured in all the horsey mags. We learned tons from that one. There was only one other pupil in the library—a geeky boy who looked like the sort who was revving up to invent a life-changing something or other. Sweet! But what should I search for? After ten minutes of dead ends, I found a hopeful site.

The site, I have to say, was mind-blowing. You'll never guess—well, honestly, you wouldn't, not in a million years so I'll have to tell you—it seems that my little statue was a tribute to an ancient goddess, no less. There were pictures on the website of figures very similar to the one Drum had stumbled on, the one tucked safely in my waistcoat pocket at home. They were uncannily similar.

"Gotcha!" I exclaimed loudly. The geeky boy didn't even look up.

My statue went by the name of Epona, a Celtic goddess who had been adopted by the Romans since she was the goddess of mares and foals, mules and the cavalry. Small statues of Epona were, the website told me, always showing

up in ancient Roman sites where Roman cavalry had been
stationed. I knew this area was riddled with Roman history
so it made sense to find something like my Epona statue.

Wow! Epona, I thought. That's your name, eh?

The bell rang, so I made my way through the corridors
to my next lesson, geography.

And that is when the *worst* and the *best* thing happened.

I had no idea where my next classroom was, but then I
spotted Catriona along the corridor with two of her friends,
so I decided to follow at a safe distance. Why is it that in
school corridors, everyone seems to be going in the opposite
direction of you? A gang of older boys appeared and were
pushing me against the wall when one of their friends, as
a joke (ha, ha, *not!*), ran up behind them, skidding on the
polished floor, bouncing off them, and cannoning into me.
I saw him coming and had nowhere to go. You know that
feeling you get when you just know you can't rescue the
day, that it's just a nightmare, and roll on to tomorrow? We
both went down on the parquet like pins and, lucky me, I
ended up underneath, pinned to the floor by a ninth-grader
who weighed at least 170 pounds. Breathe? I don't think so!

So there I was clambering about on the floor, gasping for
air with my skirt up, displaying my underwear to the whole
school, my bag and books scattered around me and amid
all the laughing and shouting and insults, someone put out
a hand to help me up. Frantically pulling my skirt down, I
looked up to see—and this was the final humiliation—none
other than James!

I thought I would die.

Is there anything worse than seeing a boy you like when you're wearing a school uniform? Well, yes. Seeing the boy you like when your school uniform is up over your face, actually. I felt myself turn double crimson, and I could have passed out on the spot.

"I thought it was you, horse whisperer!" he grinned. I didn't grin back. I was mortified and gasping like a fish out of water. "Too bad you didn't see that coming!" he joked, hauling me to my feet. And then he was gone, off with his friends down the corridor, leaving me leaning against the wall, breathless and closing my eyes in mortification. When I opened them again, I saw Catriona and her friends laughing at me before they ran off toward the classroom I would never find.

Gathering my books from the floor, I wondered what other horrible thing could happen to me today. No wonder people ditched school, I thought, considering it for the first time in my life. I could just slip out of the gates and go to the stables. No one would know. I could escape. Run away. Drummer would be waiting and we could go riding and chat.

But then something so great happened, I decided I wouldn't run anywhere. Just before he turned the corner, James looked over his shoulder and smiled at me. And instead of feeling like a smear on the wall, I felt just wonderful. How did that work? Ridiculously buoyant because of James's smile—and filing the ditching idea away for later should I need it—I got super turned around finding my geography class. Luckily, Mr. Chann, the teacher, let me off being late because I was new. And then, just as I thought it couldn't get any worse, Mr. Chann decided to continue my torture.

"OK, everyone," he said, "I want you to form groups of four for this next exercise."

I found myself in a foursome with a blond girl called Mel, a boy with glasses, and, naturally, Catriona. As we were left to our own devices, Catriona started, completely ignoring Mr. Chann's assignment about volcanoes and following her own, hateful agenda.

"How was your trip?" she smirked. "Nice underwear! I'm sure everyone in the school is sorry they missed those, but you never know how things can change."

"Well," I said, smiling sweetly, "it was nice of James to help me up. Isn't he the best?" Catriona glared at me and my heart sank. I was going to pay for that.

"Did you know that our new girl has a secret?" she said to the others, glancing at me slyly.

"What do you mean?" asked the boy with glasses.

"Come on," said Mel, "tell us!"

"Big fat liar *Mia* here *claims to be* a horse whisperer," Catriona announced, her voice heavy with sarcasm.

"Are you?" said Mel, her eyes even wider. "You mean you can talk to horses and that?"

"I thought your name was Pia?" asked the boy with glasses.

"It is," I said.

"Oh, is it? My bad," Catriona smirked.

I kept a straight face, determined not to give Catriona the satisfaction of letting her get to me.

"What do they say, the horses and that?" asked Mel, intrigued.

"Yes, *Mia*, what do they say?" echoed Catriona, mimicking Mel's voice.

"Well, your pony told me how much she hates you," I replied.

"Hey, Nadine, Cat says Pia's a horse whisperer. How cool is that?" Mel hissed to her friend on the table next to us. Nadine's eyebrows shot upward into her bangs.

"Really?" she said.

"Says Cat's horse hates her!" Mel added, and they both giggled.

Catriona looked furious. Well, I thought, you started it.

"But she can't *really* talk to them!" said Cat. She was beginning to lose control of the situation she had created.

I decided to play along. What did I have to lose? So I told Mel that, yes, I did seem to possess some strange, unexplainable way with horses and that I could indeed sense things about them, and she soaked it up! By the end of the lesson Mel had become my unofficial PR machine, and at least three girls had approached me about my magical powers.

But then, just as I was thinking I'd turned it around and I had Catriona on the run, something else happened as I made my way to the last lesson of the day:

"Nice underwear, new girl!" yelled a boy in my class, and he and his three friends all laughed.

"Have a nice trip?" two girls asked me, before sniggering and walking off.

What? How did they know about my embarrassing incident in the corridor? Then Mel enlightened me.

"Is this really you?" she asked, shoving her cell phone under my nose. And there I was, upside down with my underwear on show, snapped by Catriona who had been in the right or wrong place at the right or wrong time, depending on your point of view.

My heart sank. It sank lower and lower as my classmates—as well as pupils from other classes—smirked knowingly in my direction for the rest of the afternoon. Catriona was back on top. I felt so angry. All because I wouldn't let Bambi have Drummer's stable. What a vindictive brat! Right, I thought, this was war—and I wasn't beaten yet!

At last, the bell rang and everyone tore out of the school gates. No one tore out quicker than me and I raced to the yard to change into my riding clothes and meet up with Drum who was waiting for me in his stable.

"Where have you been, you slacker? I've been bored stiff all day," he said, shaking his head and pinning his ears to his neck, pretending to look evil to emphasize his point.

"Sorry," I said, patting his neck, "but I've had a bad day—"

"Don't do that, I hate it," he interrupted irritably. "You can rub my ears if you like," he added meekly. "I like that."

"But I *always* pet your neck."

"I know, and I *always* hate it! Am I going out in the field tonight? *Do* say yes," he continued dramatically.

"Yes," I replied. "I want to be there when you go out for the first time, in case you don't get along with the other ponies and I have to rescue you." School was forgotten for the time being.

Drummer just looked at me like I was an idiot. "What makes you think I won't get along with the others? You're the one with that type of problem, not me."

"You are the rudest pony I have ever had a conversation with," I told him.

"Just turn me out in the field and then go and get on with your humdrum life," he replied.

"No way, Sunshine, we're going riding first. I've had a bad day, too."

Drummer groaned. "Oh, boohoo. It's all about you, isn't it?!"

We went in the woods and every time I asked him to canter, Drum bucked. So, feeling mean after my school experience, I dug my knees in, shoved my heels down and my shoulders back, and told him we weren't going back until he behaved himself, taking him for a blast along the bridle paths and around the fields. Then, when he got too tired to buck anymore, we headed home.

"That was great, Drum," I said, patting his neck.

"I have asked you *not* to do that," Drummer puffed.

"Oops, sorry. I'll rub the top of your mane, instead."

"Mmmm, that's OK. Up a bit…down a bit…just there needs a little rub," Drummer replied, sticking his head in the air and poking his nose as I scratched an itch for him.

We arrived back to discover that most of the other ponies were already out in the field. Only Moth and the rug-swathed brownish-gray pony belonging to earrings girl were still in. I felt quite sorry for the brownish-gray pony; it was pretty hot to be wearing a rug. As I led Drum past the empty loose boxes toward the field, I rubbed his black-tipped ears. It's always a bit anxious turning your beloved pony out with strangers the first time. Would they get along? Would they fight? Would Drum pal up with anyone? I could feel my heart thumping for Drummer. It would be like my first day at school, only worse. Ponies never hold back—Drummer could get hurt by flying hooves belonging to jealous ponies, unwilling to accept the new boy. He could have a much rougher time than I had at school.

I gulped as we reached the gate. Bambi and Tiffany were grazing together, Dolly was over by the water trough, and the blue roan and a chunky, black native pony stood by the far fence with a tiny bay pony and a rather stunning liver chestnut horse. As I led Drum through the gate, I saw Dolly lift her head. She'd be thrilled to see Drum at least. But what about the others?

Unbuckling the halter, I gave Drummer a big kiss on the nose.

"Be careful," I whispered.

"Yuck!" spat Drummer. "Must you? In front of everyone? Are you *trying* to get me beaten up? Just go, for goodness' sake. I'll be fine!"

"Oh, go on then!" I said. He really was the most ungrateful pony, *ever!*

Holding my breath, I leaned over the gate and watched Dolly canter over.

"Oh, at last!" she said, arching her dappled neck. "Hi there, handsome. Come on, I'll show you around. The trough's over there, the field shelter is up the far side—but quite frankly it needs cleaning out, so no one's bothering to go in there right now—and we've made a fantastic dust-bath rolling patch I can show you. We can share a dust-bath if you like. You've met Bambi and Tiffany, of course…" She looked over toward them and Bambi and Tiffany nodded an acknowledgement. "But you haven't met Bluey and Henry, and that's Pippin, the oldest pony here, and Lester, who comes to shows with me."

I watched with my heart in my mouth as Drummer, Bluey, and the black native pony Henry snorted up one another's nostrils while senior citizen Pippin, the tiny bay with a white blaze and two white socks, and the handsome liver chestnut Lester looked on. This could be when a fight broke out. But, no, I heard Drummer introduce himself, heard Bluey welcome him to the gang, and watched as they all meandered off into the sunset like they'd been mates all their lives.

What? No, really, I mean, *what?* If only my first day at school had been like that (without the snorting up the nostrils bit, of course). How come ponies had it so figured out? How come people were so, so…difficult? What was I doing wrong? I suddenly remembered about Epona—I'd forgotten to tell Drum the news about our goddess. Never mind, it would wait.

I took myself back to the yard to clean out Drummer's stable. James's pony Moth was next door, looking out over her half door. I secretly grinned to myself as I remembered James smiling at me at school.

"Hi, Moth," I whispered, going to stroke her white face. But she quickly backed away into her stable and stood in the farthest corner, facing me suspiciously. Leaning over the door, I held out my hand with a couple of pony nuts in my palm.

"Here, girl," I said softly, "here's some treats for you." But Moth turned her face to the wall and ignored me. She didn't even say anything. I was starting to get used to hearing what the ponies said, but Moth said nothing. She wasn't giving anything away. It was strange, I thought. Why was Moth so quiet? It was as though she couldn't bear to see me.

I left her alone.

As Drummer had been in all day, it took me forever to clean out his stable. I checked on him again before leaving the yard and was amused to see him grazing nose to nose with Dolly. Now he was out there, she wasn't going to let him out of her sight!

"'Night, Drummer," I called.

"Yeah, whatever..." Drummer mumbled between mouthfuls of grass, not bothering to lift his head.

Moth was looking out over her half door again as I collected my bike and pedaled down the drive, passing a car driven by James's father, with James in the seat beside him. It looked like a perfectly ordinary car, I thought, not the sort of car a long-lost heir or a gypsy prince would be driven around in—but then, what did I know about cars? James gave me a wave as they drove by. Double pooh! If I'd stayed another two minutes, we'd have been alone together! I couldn't go back. I wondered how Moth would be with her owner. Would she be so standoffish with him?

Feeling like a spy, I jumped off my bike at the end of the drive and, hiding in the bushes, I peered around a leafy branch to see James get out of the car and walk toward Moth's stable. As he got nearer, Moth did exactly as she had with me, hastily backing away from the stable door and disappearing into her stable.

Well, that's odd, I thought to myself. Drummer always strained over his door trying to get at the apple or carrot I always took for him. Most ponies frisked you for a treat or even just wanted to talk to you. I couldn't think of one pony that acted like Moth.

As I pedaled home, I couldn't stop thinking about what I'd seen. Why was Moth so unwilling to interact with people—even James? Why wouldn't she talk to me when I couldn't get any of the other ponies to shut up? The very beginnings of an unwelcome suspicion started to grow and fester. I didn't want to go there, I really didn't, but the suspicion had a life of its own, and I was powerless to stop it. It niggled and niggled, and I knew that before long, I would have to pay attention to it, dig it out, and examine it. And I didn't want to do that because I was scared of what I might discover. What I might discover about James.

CHAPTER 5

THE WEEKEND CAME AT last. When I woke up on Saturday morning, I leaped out of bed to check the weather (sunny—yippee!) before galloping downstairs for breakfast. Dressed and out the door in record time, I arrived at the stables just in time to say hi to Mrs. Collins and pet Squish, grab Drummer's halter, and head off to the field before anyone else showed up to spoil things. Of course, I had Epona in my pocket. She had become a permanent fixture.

In the field, a low-lying mist drifted around the ponies' legs, making them look like fairy horses flying on clouds. Drummer had settled in so well with all his new pals, he turned a little sour at the thought of me dragging him away from them.

"Is it the weekend already?" he moaned, screwing up his black nose and twitching his red ears in disgust. Some fairy horse.

"Come on," I said, slipping on his halter and giving him an apple, "let's go riding before it gets all busy with walkers and small children and dogs swarming all over the bridle paths."

"Get it out of the way, I suppose," mused Drum. "See you, guys!" he yelled. The other ponies murmured their farewells, and we wandered over the gate just as Katy, the girl with red hair and a zillion freckles, arrived on the other side of it. She wore her hair pulled back with a lilac ribbon in a ponytail, and she was dressed in a lilac polo shirt with purple jodhpurs. A purple halter swung from one hand.

"Ask her whether she likes purple," Drummer mumbled, making me stifle a giggle.

"Oh, hello," said Katy.

"Hi," I replied, hesitantly. I was still suspicious of anyone talking to me.

"Your Drummer is so cute; he's part Arab, isn't he?" she asked, opening the gate and letting herself into the field. Cute? That's all she knew, I thought.

"Yes," I replied, patting Drummer's neck. He let out a huge sigh and I remembered—he didn't like that. My hands went to his ears and I pulled them gently instead.

"Your pony is the blue roan, isn't it?" I asked. The pony was already walking over to her. At least he was pleased to see his owner. "He's a lovely color," I said. And he was. Blue roans have a mixture of black and white hair, so they look sort of speckly. In the winter their bodies go pale gray, with black legs, mane, and tail, but now, the pony's summer coat was almost black, with gray flecks throughout and a bluish-gray head and tummy.

"Mmmm, I love his color and the way he changes with the seasons," Katy told me. "Is that right you're a horse whisperer? Dee and Bean are telling everyone you are. Is it true?"

Drummer snorted. "Horse whisperer, my…"

"Well, sort of," I agreed. There was no turning back now, not after playing along at school. And besides, I reminded myself, I was at war with Catriona, and me being a horse whisperer annoyed her.

"That is *so* exciting!" Katy said, and her ponytail wobbled up and down as she shrugged her shoulders. "I suppose it's something you're born with, like being a clairvoyant?"

"Mmmm, probably," I agreed, giving Drummer a look. He was rolling his eyes upward.

The roan reached us. "This is Bluey," Katy announced, fastening his purple halter around his ears and turning to walk with us. Together, we trooped into the yard, parting to go to our separate stables—Drummer to the right, Bluey to the left. As soon as Drummer got inside, he started.

"Honestly, how can you keep a straight face? *Horse whisperer!*"

"I can hear *you* well enough," I said.

"Only with your little magic friend."

"Oh, yes, I forgot; I found out all about it!" I told him, pulling the statue of Epona out of my pocket and looking at it again. "She's a *goddess*, the goddess of horses, and her name's Epona. Don't ask me how, but she's responsible for letting me hear you—and the others, of course."

"How?"

"I said don't ask…I thought you could hear me?"

"Well, I think you should put her back or in a safe place. You shouldn't be carrying it around with you all the time,"

Drummer said, rummaging around in his stall. "Am I on a diet?"

"If I didn't have her with me, I wouldn't be able to hear you…or the others!"

"Precisely!"

"And actually," I added spitefully, "you are looking a bit on the pudgy side."

"Who are you talking to?" Drummer and I jumped guiltily as Katy looked over the stable door.

"Er, just Drummer. I always talk to Drummer," I said, truthfully.

"I talk to Bluey, too. Sometimes I think it would be great if he could talk back." Katy sighed.

I wouldn't be too sure about that, I thought, tucking Epona away in my pocket again. She was my good luck charm, my passport to making friends and, who could tell, possibly even fame and fortune!

I groomed at top speed, determined to go riding before Catriona showed up. I was supposed to give Drummer at least an hour to rest after grazing in the field all night, but if we took it steady, I knew it would be all right. Getting him ready, I led him out to discover Katy mounted on Bluey—and the purple theme continued in Bluey's browband and saddlecloth. The pope would have looked understated by comparison. I wondered why Katy didn't go for blue; it made sense, what with her pony's color and name and all.

"Going for a ride?" I asked her.

"No, I'm schooling Bluey for a dressage competition next weekend," Katy said.

"Do you like dressage?" Drummer asked Bluey. "Personally, I can't stand it!"

"Neither can I!" Bluey replied, chewing on his bit and flicking his ears back and forth. "I'm a cross-country pony, only Katy doesn't know it. She never wants to do it—won't even try it with me. I think she had a scare with her last pony. I'd take care of her, though. If you want to go cross-country in total safety, Bluey is your pony. But instead, I have to go around and around in endless circles. Boring!"

Poor old Bluey, I thought, having overheard.

"Do you like dressage, Katy?" I asked.

"Not much. I used to enjoy jumping cross-country, but my last pony put in a couple of nasty stops and I fell onto some jumps and hurt myself. That's why I got Bluey here. He's a bit of a plodder so he's given me back my confidence. He's no jumper, though. Too chunky to get off the ground, I would think!" She laughed and patted Bluey affectionately.

"See?" wailed Bluey. "She totally doesn't get it. Plodder indeed! I'm an ace at cross-country and I never stop. Not the fastest, but the *bravest*. My mom was legendary; on all the Pony Club teams, she was. If only Katy would give me a chance."

Drummer gave me one of his looks. "Go on then," he urged, "do your so-called horse whispering thing and sort this one out. I know you're bursting to."

Of course!

61

"Katy, Bluey is actually *dying* to go jumping cross-country. He's a really good cross-country pony and he'd never stop with you."

"Yeah, right!" said Katy. "Honestly, Pia, you don't know Bluey. He's just not cross-country material—and I really can't chance it. I'm too nervous."

Then it came to me: if I wanted to make this work for me, if I wanted people to buy into the fact that I could hear horses and ride on the back of it, I needed to jazz it up a bit. Put on a show. Give it a bit of pizzazz! I put my hands on Bluey's neck, half closing my eyes and sighing deeply. Bluey rolled his eyes at me, then back toward Drummer. His ears went into overdrive, back and forth, back and forth.

"What's her game?" he snorted.

"Wish I knew," Drummer replied, yawning.

I started nodding my head. "I understand," I whispered, loud enough for Katy to hear.

"Get your head-case human off me," Bluey hissed.

"Yeah, like I can do anything. She's a loose cannon, dude. I have to put up with it every day."

"Yes," I said, "I know…cross-country is what you love to do, you were *born* to do. I'll try to make your feelings understood." My voice had gone all sort of weird fortune-tellerish. Deep and dramatic. I wondered whether I'd overdone it—it clearly needed work.

"Wow!" Katy whispered, her eyes wide, her jaw dropping. "Are you doing your horse whispering thing? Is Bluey communicating with you? Tell me!"

"He longs to go cross-country jumping. He'll look after you. He only asks that you give him a chance to prove himself," I said. I could do this—piece of cake!

"Really?" asked Katy. "I mean, honest? Bluey? *My* Bluey? Are you sure?" She looked at her pony carefully, like she'd never really seen him before.

"Why don't you try it?" I suggested in my normal voice, backing away from Bluey. The blue roan shuddered like ponies do when they're shaking off an annoying fly.

"She's nuts," he said to Drummer, "and I don't understand how she can hear me."

"You said it," Drummer replied, "she's nuts!"

Katy looked at me and then at Bluey. Pressing her lips together and taking a deep breath, she took a huge leap of faith and made a decision.

"I'm going to give it a try right now!" she cried, shortening her stirrups to jumping length. "Would you come with me—give me your moral support?"

I almost fell over. Katy was inviting me to ride with her. A first! This horse whispering gig really was working for me. I felt Epona in my pocket. My lucky charm!

"Sure," I replied, trying to sound all cool. I felt ridiculously happy about it. At last I had someone to ride with. I mounted Drummer and we all headed off to the woods where there were plenty of cross-country jumps just waiting to be tackled by Bluey. At last.

"I'd never thought of Bluey as the cross-country type," Katy told me as we rode along. "Nobody ever has. He's a bit chunky and quite lazy. He's never shown any enthusiasm for show jumping…"

"I'm going cross-country, I'm going cross-country!" Bluey sang.

"So I hope you're right, Pia. If he stops and I fall off…" Katy trailed off.

I hoped I was right, too. But how could I not be? Bluey was getting so excited.

Drummer wasn't. "I hope you don't expect me to dash around after Red Rum, here," he moaned.

"Stop whining!" I said.

"I'm not whining!" replied Katy. "I'm really going to give it a chance."

"Not you," I explained. "Drummer. He's always whining," I added, pointedly.

"I am *not!*" Drummer exclaimed. "I'm merely telling it like it is."

"Is he?" asked Katy, looking at Drummer. "He looks so sweet. I can't imagine him whining; he's so gorgeous."

"See?" said Drummer, in his best smug voice. "I'm gorgeous!"

"Bambi doesn't think so," I said, being mean. Drummer said nothing—which was a first. I took it he was sulking.

We reached the jumps. Bluey started to dance around on his toes; he couldn't help himself.

"I'm going jumping, I'm going jumping, I'm going jumping, I'm going—"

"Well, go on then!" interrupted Drummer. "You're giving me a headache!"

"Oh, Bluey," squeaked Katy, astonished. "You really want to do it, don't you? Well, OK then, but take it steady."

"Have fun!" I shouted to Katy, as she headed Bluey to the first fence, a log pile.

Squealing with excitement, Bluey bounced into a canter, popping over the log pile and speeding onto the next jump, transformed from a chunky workhorse into a cross-country pony.

"Wow!" exclaimed Drummer, looking after Bluey with his head up and his little red ears pricked forward. "Look at him *go!* Wears me out just looking at him."

"Oh, he's so happy." I sighed. The horse whispering thing was such fun! I could really help horses, really make a difference. I saw my future as a famous horse whisperer. I could do demonstrations, fill huge arenas, go on TV. People would flock to hear my wisdom. My future as a horsey celebrity was assured. This was so exciting! Good old Epona. What a find!

Bluey came back drenched in sweat and still dancing on his toes. Katy's face was like a split melon, with a huge beam of a smile.

"That was *awesome!*" she cried, patting her pony like crazy. "Bluey was just fantastic. He loved it—and so did I! It was just like it was before I fell off and lost my nerve. We're going to have a lot of fun."

"Have yourself a good time, did you?" asked Drummer.

"The best!" puffed Bluey. "You don't know what it's like to be labeled a plodder when you're just dying to show everyone that there's more to you than they think."

65

"You know they'll never let you stop now, don't you?" Drummer said.

"Bring it on!" puffed Bluey.

Katy patted her wet pony again, wiping Bluey's sweat from her hand onto her purple jodhpurs. "I'd better walk him for a while," she said. "He's sweating due to excitement more than effort. Can I come for a ride with you? I'm going to see where we can enter for some competitions. Want to come?" she asked.

"See, I told you," groaned Drummer.

"You're just scared you'll have to do some work. I can't wait!" Bluey said, sighing with contentment.

We had a great ride. It was just so nice to go riding with someone at last. Drummer and Bluey got on well and Katy showed me a couple of paths through the woods that I hadn't known about and told me some gossip, too.

"How are you getting on in Shelly's old stable?" she asked. "Has Cat calmed down yet—you know she wanted to claim that for Bambi, don't you?"

"Yes, she made that quite plain," I answered, remembering our confrontation and my refusal to move Drummer to Bambi's stable.

"So I started off slowly over the log pile to give Katy confidence..." began Bluey to Drummer.

"Can you guess why she wanted to move Bambi?" Katy continued, pushing an eye-level branch out of the way and letting it ping back behind her.

I decided to play dumb. "No," I said, "I haven't the faintest idea. She didn't say."

"…then I cranked it up over the ditch, cantering up the hill to the step jump, where I…" continued Bluey.

Katy laughed. "Cat likes James. She's crazy about him."

"Really?" I said, trying to sound surprised. I hoped I wasn't going red. Cat wasn't alone. I mean, honestly, who wouldn't like James?

"…then down over the other side to the brush fence, which I flew…"

"Do talk me through it, jump by jump, why don't you?" Drummer mumbled.

"She thinks she's in with a chance—after all, one of her brothers is his best friend. He's always around her house," said Katy.

This was news. I told myself it didn't matter. But it did. I imagined James hanging around my house, with a brother I didn't have. How cool would that be?

"So they're not going out, then?" I asked, casually. Bluey was still boring Drummer, but with this bit of news about Catriona's brother being James's best friend, I blocked it out.

"No. No way. James *was* going out with a girl from school—oh, I saw you at school the other day, but we're in different classes, so you were miles away. I don't suppose our paths will cross much."

"I didn't know you went to that school!" I said.

"Well, like I said, we're unlikely to see much of each other," Katy said. "Cat sent me a photo of you on my cell phone; you were flat on your back near the science block. Tough break!"

My heart sank. "The tough part was that Catriona was there when it happened. I'm getting no end of looks from everyone wherever I go."

"Someone's started a caption competition for it, I don't know who," Katy continued.

Could it get any worse?

"The winner at the moment is something like…let me see…er…that's it, *Recognize anyone you know?* I think that's it. I can't remember now."

Yes, it could.

Bluey and Drummer walked on a long rein in step with each other.

"Did I tell you how I negotiated the tricky drop jump?" asked Bluey.

"Only twice." Drummer sighed.

"Is Bluey happy now?" asked Katy. She obviously loved Bluey to bits.

"He's so happy, he could burst," I told her, truthfully. What a hoot!

The hoot fizzled out when we got back to the yard for as we pulled up outside Drummer's stable, I noticed that Catriona was grooming Bambi in the stable next door, and Pippin, the ancient bay pony, was being bounced about on by a tiny child with fair hair. Her mother was leading Pippin up and down the yard while the little girl squealed with delight.

"We'll have to go riding again soon," Katy suggested.

"Please, no!" exclaimed Drummer.

"That would be great," I said, dismounting and glaring at Drummer.

"Thanks again, Pia," said Katy, rubbing Bluey's forehead. "I can't believe how great you are, Bluey," she whispered, giving him a hug.

Before I could put Drummer in his stable, Dee's mom ran across the yard to us, highly excited.

"Oh, Pia, I'm glad you're here. I've some very exciting news for you…"

I looked at her blankly, but she raved on.

"I have a friend who works for the *Bretstone Herald*, a reporter, and I was talking to her all about how you saved Dolly's life that night when she had colic…"

"Well," I started, nervously, "that might be an exaggeration…"

"And she's very interested in doing a piece on you," Dee's mom continued.

"What do you mean," I said, "a piece?"

"Interview you. Just a small piece, I imagine; so don't get too excited. I told her how you helped with Tiffany, too. My friend is very interested in horse whispering—it's all the rage with the media at the moment."

"Not another one who believes this horse whispering stuff!" cried Catriona, leaning over her stable, dandy brush in hand.

"What do you mean?" asked Dee's mom.

"*Lia* here is making it up. I can't believe you're all taken in by her!"

"Her name is Pia, dear," Dee's mom said.

"I can understand you being suspicious, Cat," began Katy, diplomatically, "but only this morning Pia told me that Bluey loves cross-country—and she was right! We went around the jumps in the woods and Bluey flew around like one of Pippa Funnell's horses. I would never have known if Pia hadn't done her horse whispering thing on him," she said.

"What horse whispering thing? What did she do?" asked Catriona, glaring at me.

"Yes," echoed Dee's mom, "tell us everything."

By this time, Pippin's little entourage had wandered over and the mother was listening. There was quite an audience.

"Well," Katy started, dramatically, "Pia laid her hands on his neck and Bluey told her how much he wanted to go cross-country jumping. It was miraculous! I would never have known. And it felt fantastic. I feel like I've got my nerve back. All because of Pia here. She's amazing."

"Goodness, did you hear that, Bethany?" said the child's mom. The child giggled and bounced a bit more. I heard Pippin sigh—but then, I realized, so did everyone.

"Wonderful!" enthused Dee's mom, ignoring Catriona. "It's tremendously exciting having our very own horse whisperer. When can my reporter friend come and interview you? She'll be very interested in hearing about Bluey, too."

"She'll be wasting her time," grumbled Catriona. "Lia's no more a horse whisperer than I'm Ellen Whitaker. She won't do it because she's *not* a horse whisperer. She'll look stupid."

Well, I had to do it now! Besides, I had wanted to be a celeb—this could swing it.

"How about one evening next week?" I heard myself saying, coolly.

One phone call later and the interview was fixed for Monday evening. I curled my fingers around Epona and wondered how it would feel to be a local celebrity. Catriona could stick that on her cell phone and send it to anyone she liked. Then I remembered that she liked James, which made me all the more determined to get her wound up.

I was fighting back!

CHAPTER 6

WE HAD A GREAT weekend, Drummer and me. After our ride with Katy and Bluey, Katy and I cleaned tack together, sitting on upturned buckets outside Bluey's stable—opposite Drum's row of three. It wasn't long before Dee joined us, munching on a chocolate bar and twirling her hair around her fingers.

"We'll fill you in on some of the others at the yard," said Katy, dumping her stirrup irons in a bucket of water, and she told me that Leanne's dun pony was called Mr. Higgins. They competed in dressage—mainly, Katy said, because Leanne's boyfriend, Stuart, competed in dressage, too. Only he had a whopping great chestnut Danish Warmblood horse that he kept at home and was trained by a top trainer (real fancy shmancy) and was always getting picked for the older, more serious Pony Club teams. Leanne and Mr. Higgins were much more low-key apparently, but Katy thought they'd probably go the same way.

"And, of course," Dee said, flicking her brown hair out of her eyes, "Catriona hangs around with Leanne 'cause Leanne moves in the right circles. It's all right for Leanne, she can afford it, but Cat can't. She'll never be able to have another horse. I wish I could get my hair cut," she added.

"Once Bambi goes back, she'll have to beg rides off everyone," Katy said, picking Bluey grease off her saddle with her nails. "Why *don't* you get your hair cut? You're always complaining about it."

Hang on, hang on, I thought. Rewind! What was that little snippet I'd almost missed? "What do you mean?" I asked.

"Dee's always going on about her hair," Katy replied. "Just go and get it done, will you? The students at Supercuts will do it for you for nothing on a Tuesday night. I'll come with you."

"No, I mean about Bambi, about her going back. Go back where?" That sounded much more interesting than Dee's hairdressing problem, but Dee didn't think so.

"I can't get it cut because Mom insists on it being long enough to wear in a braid or a bun when I'm in the show ring," grumbled Dee.

I looked at Katy. "Bambi?" I repeated. Katy went a bit pink.

"Oh, I didn't mean anything," she said, a little too hastily. "Cat just loves Bambi a lot, that's all. She wouldn't want a Warmblood."

There was something she was hiding, but I couldn't *make* her tell me. Besides, I didn't want to sound too interested in knowing, in case she told Catriona.

"Then there's Mrs. Bradley," continued Katy. "She's about a hundred years old and owns Henry, the black Dales pony stabled around the corner. Bless him, he does exactly what he likes with Mrs. B. Wipes the floor with her," Katy explained.

"James once said that Henry would have the perfect pony life if he could just go deaf!" giggled Dee. "Mrs. B's always squeaking at him," she explained to me. "Oh, I think that's a split end," she added, still examining her hair. "Now it will *have* to be cut!"

Grateful that someone had brought up the subject of James—and not just so we could get off the wretched subject of Dee's hair—I thought carefully about how I could ask Katy about Moth's suspect behavior.

"What's the story behind James and Moth?" I asked, wringing out my dirty sponge in the bucket. The question was deliberately ambiguous and I wondered how Katy would answer.

"Mmmm, funny you should ask," said Katy. My heart thudded in my chest. Katy knew something. "Moth just arrived one day, without anyone expecting a new livery. James had to find somewhere fast, apparently. It was a bit of a mystery. Exciting, though!"

"He was a bit off at first, though," remembered Dee. "Not very friendly with anyone but Cat. He's better now."

Aha! I thought. Probably had to leave his previous yard under a cloud; no doubt someone there had noticed Moth's timid behavior. I couldn't understand why no one else seemed to suspect anything, unless they chose not to discuss it with the new girl, me. And there was the Cat connection. What was that about? Drummer chose that moment to neigh across the yard and interrupt my thoughts. At least, that's what everyone else heard. I heard...

"Hey! Any chance of going back out in the field? The grass won't eat itself, you know!"

"I think Drummer wants out," I said, getting to my feet. "Is Bluey going out with him?"

Katy peered over Bluey's door. "Mmmm, I think he's dry now," she said. "I'll come with you."

We turned the ponies out and watched them roll before tearing at the grass. Is there anything more relaxing than watching ponies—particularly your own pony—grazing? I don't think so. I could watch Drummer for ages. Except that I had his tack to finish. So we went back and scrubbed and polished until both saddles and bridles were gleaming. It had been a good morning.

On Sunday, I schooled Drummer early before galloping back home to help Mom tidy up the garden. It was a huge mess—all overgrown—so we worked and worked and after an afternoon of scratches and stings from roses and nettles, we finally had it tamed. Thank goodness it's only a small garden!

I don't quite know why I didn't mention the impending interview to Mom. The right moment didn't present itself. Then I sort of forgot. Then, by the time it was Monday evening, it seemed a bit late. And we didn't get the *Bretstone Herald* anyway, and Dee's mom had said it was only going to be a small piece, so I thought it was hardly worth mentioning. So I didn't. I thought I'd wait until my celebrity status was more high profile. Actually, it wasn't *just* that; I had this feeling that Mom wouldn't approve, so I didn't want her to ask lots of awkward questions about me hearing ponies or saying I couldn't do the interview. I thought I just wouldn't bring it up.

After school (not so bad as last week—the cell phone thing had died down, thank goodness), I put on my favorite pink jodhpurs and striped top, shoved Epona in my pocket, and raced past Mom, who was glued to the Internet again, with a cheery, "See you later!"

A reception committee was waiting for me at the yard and Drummer was already in from the field.

"I brought him in for you, to save you time," said Katy.

"We all groomed him, so he'll look great in the photographs," added Bean.

What photographs? I thought, noticing that Catriona was nowhere to be seen.

"We didn't think you'd want to get dirty," finished Dee. "I mean, it's all right for us; we're not the ones being interviewed."

You could have fooled me. Everyone seemed to be wearing their best gear—all clean, of course. But then, I had to admit, they had been kind enough to get my celebrity pony ready.

I looked at my celebrity pony. My celebrity pony stared back at me. Drummer had been brushed and scrubbed and his mane and forelock had been slicked down with a damp brush. He looked a bit like a small boy who'd been reluctantly spruced up for a visit from relatives.

"Thanks ever so much!" I said, stifling a giggle. Drum looked furious.

"I've been attacked!" he growled. "They all came at me with brushes. I didn't stand a chance. And so *rude*—cleaning bits they have no right to clean!" He didn't have time to go on, however, because an unknown car came bouncing down the drive—the reporter had arrived. I felt really nervous and put my hands behind me, in case they were shaking. This celebrity thing was scary!

Caroline Simpson was about Mom's age. Short. Lots of wild dark hair. Glasses. Jeans and a white T-shirt. Red scarf tied around her neck like a cowboy. Notebook, pen. Earnest.

"Hello," she said in a breathless voice that sounded like autumn leaves blowing across a pavement. "Caroline Simpson, *Bretstone Herald*. I've come to see Pia."

Everyone parted before her like the Red Sea had for Moses, leaving me and Drummer in full view. Caroline Simpson pushed her glasses onto the back of her nose with one finger and extended her hand, clearly expecting me to shake it. So I did.

"I'm Pia," I said. My mouth felt dry and my voice sounded funny. I could feel my heart thumping. I couldn't believe how nervous I felt and I wished everyone would go away. Caroline Simpson obviously thought the same.

"Could I have some time with Pia, alone?" she asked, beaming at everyone. "I'd be very grateful if I could get some quotes from you all later."

The others nodded and melted away—but only to the other side of the yard where they hovered outside Dolly's stable, pretending not to stare at us.

"Wow, get a load of her!" said Drummer. "The press, no less!"

"Shhh!" I whispered, closing my eyes and holding my breath when I realized what I'd done.

"Pardon?" said Caroline Simpson.

"Sorry, not you, er…"

Caroline Simpson narrowed her eyes. "Are you doing it now?" she asked, flicking her notepad open and clicking on her pen. "Are you talking to your lovely pony here?"

"This is Drummer," I said.

"He's gorgeous," Caroline Simpson enthused, smiling broadly. I warmed to her a bit—after all, Drum *is* gorgeous.

"When did you first discover you had this gift, this gift of talking with horses and ponies?" she continued.

"Quite recently," I said.

"And how does it work? I understand the ponies tell you things that trouble them. You saved Sophie's top show pony, Dolly Daydream, from certain death?"

"Well," I started, "Dolly had colic and I happened to be passing…"

"And you saved the dear pony from certain death," Caroline Simpson repeated, writing something down. She seemed fixated on me saving a pony from certain death.

"And Sophie tells me you discovered a pony's talent for cross-country, something of which its rider was unaware?" she continued.

"Who the muck heap is Sophie?" interjected Drummer. I supposed Sophie was Dee's mom.

"Well, Bluey—the pony—told me he liked jumping cross-country, but his owner Katy didn't know anything about it," I explained, starting to get into the swing of it. If I wanted to be a celebrity, I had to wake up a bit. "He's so happy about it, too," I added, smiling.

"What motivates you to do this horse whispering?" Caroline Simpson asked, scribbling away. She peered at me intently, clearly expecting much. Come on, Pia, I thought, what would she want to hear? What would a horse whispering celebrity say? My mind went blank. Then I wondered what would wind Catriona up.

"I suppose I just want to make a difference, to help horses and ponies," I explained, earnestly. That sounded good, I thought.

"Oh, *puh-leese!*" chortled Drummer, stifling a laugh.

"I love the cute snuffly noises your lovely pony makes," gushed Caroline Simpson, smiling at Drum. "And is it something you're born with?" she continued, turning back to me. "I mean, has anyone else in your family ever shown any aptitude for such a vocation?"

I didn't understand most of that sentence, but I decided that a horse whisperer would, so I winged it.

"I'm the first in my family to have this, this..." I struggled for words.

"Gift?" suggested Caroline Simpson, her pen poised above her pad.

I nodded. "Well, yes, I suppose you could call it that."

Drummer snorted. I ignored him.

"So how does it work? What do you do?"

Time for some theatrics. I laid my hands on Drummer's neck. "It's strongest when I can touch the pony," I lied, "although I can hear them communicating with me without having to make any contact." This was easy!

Caroline Simpson nodded furiously. "What has your own darling pony told you? What is he saying now?"

My own darling pony said something totally unrepeatable.

"He says he's proud of me and very excited that my gift will be made public. He thinks it should be shared so that other ponies can benefit." I impressed myself thinking that line up on the spur of the moment. Drummer didn't seem to agree. Aiming a sneeze in my direction, he blew black snot all over my best pink jodhpurs. What a darling pony!

"How do you feel when you are hearing the poor, troubled ponies talk to you?" Caroline Simpson asked, her head to one side.

"Oh, well, I sometimes go into a sort of trance, but most of the time I feel a tingling in my arms and legs. It's like no other feeling in the world," I continued. I was off now, making all sorts of things up. I might as well, I thought, you only get one chance at being a celebrity.

"What *are* you going on about?" snorted Drummer.

"It's OK, Drummer," I said soothingly. I turned to Caroline Simpson. "He's a bit worried that you'll leave him out of the interview. He's very insecure. He loves his neck being patted, though. Perhaps you could do that and reassure him?"

"Oh, poor baby," crooned Caroline Simpson, briskly getting to work on Drummer, who winced theatrically every time her hand connected with his neck.

"He loves that!" I said, aiming a plastic smile at Drum. "The harder, the better!"

Fed up with thumping Drummer's neck, Caroline Simpson said she'd like to get some quotes from my friends, and she walked briskly over to the party outside Dolly's stable. Dolly was beside herself.

"Oh, the press. Tell her I almost died. Tell her I won a big class at Peterborough last week. Tell her I'm Drummer's girlfriend. Tell her that. It's very important!"

Not being much of a horse whisperer herself, Caroline Simpson ignored Dolly but instead spoke earnestly to Dee. She scribbled frantically, her red scarf bobbing like a flag as she listened to Katy; she nodded as Bean told her about Tiffany. She asked me about each *of the cases*, as she called them, and I told her what I thought she wanted to hear: how I had felt Dolly's pain, how Bluey had longed to go cross-country jumping and how happy he was now, how distressed Tiffany had been about her noseband, and how by helping Tiffany, I had helped Bean—sorry, Charlotte—too. It was a rewarding experience, I said. I considered it my duty to help. Everyone around nodded in agreement, thrilled at being included. It was a surreal experience—even without Dolly getting hysterical.

"*Tell her* all those things I just said!" she cried, rocking from one front leg to the other over her stable door, causing

Dee to shoo everyone away because her mother would freak out big-time if she saw Dolly weaving from side to side like a pendulum, as weaving is such an awful and dreaded vice.

"I think I have enough, now, thank you all so very much," gushed Caroline Simpson, snapping her notebook shut and beaming at everyone. "I just need to get a photograph of you, Pia. With Drummer would be best, I think." She walked briskly back to her car, swapping her notebook for a camera.

I fetched Drummer's nice clean bridle and put it on.

"That patting trick was just mean," he grumbled as I fastened the throatlatch, and I wondered how tight I would have to pull it to stop him whining. "I'm not going to put my ears forward now," he added.

"If you don't, you'll come out looking like an old donkey," I told him, watching his ears plop forward as he realized I had him.

We posed. We smiled. We changed poses. We smiled again. I put my arms around Drummer's neck. He gritted his teeth and nuzzled me. It was like a wedding, and we were the not-so-happy couple. *Click, click, click* and that was it. Caroline Simpson thanked us very much, told me I was fascinating, and left.

Mmmm, I mused with a pang of guilty conscience, a fascinating *liar*. Only a small piece, Dee's mom had said. Oh, well, I thought, who knew where it could lead? As it turned out, it was just as well I didn't have a crystal ball.

CHAPTER 7

WHEN I GOT HOME on Friday evening, Mom was waiting for me in the kitchen. Her lips were pressed together, her arms folded in front of her. There appeared to be a problem. There was. It was me.

"Is there something you'd like to tell me, Pia?" Mom said. Her hands moved to her hips and even a microorganism with dust for brains would have detected that she was not a happy camper. I gulped.

"Er…"

"Something about being *in the newspaper?*"

Oh. Oh, no. Oh, *pooh!*

"I can explain…" I started. My voice was a sort of squeak.

"Good. Because I'd like to hear it. How come the first I hear of you being in the newspaper is when Carol phones me this afternoon to say, '*Oh, Sue, babe, your Pia's sort of a local celebrity, isn't she?*' And what's all this about being able to talk to horses?" Her arms were folded again, her eyes blazing. Why hadn't I told her? I was sooo, *sooo* stupid. And I sooo, *sooo* hated Carol. She has to know *everything*.

"I thought you'd be pleased, a famous daughter and everything," I mumbled. It sounded lame, even to me. Clearly, *pleased* did not describe how my mom felt.

I was sent out to find a copy of the *Bretstone Herald* and when I finally tracked one down in a local news dealer, I almost fell down with shock. There was a picture of Drum and me on the front page under the headline LOCAL GIRL TALKS TO HORSES. FULL STORY, PAGE 3. It must have been a slow news week.

I gulped and gingerly opened the paper to page three. There we were, Drum and me (Drum looked gorgeous and someone at the paper had managed to airbrush the pony snot from my jodhpurs), and there was an article spanning almost the whole page. PIA, BRETSTONE'S VERY OWN PONY WHISPERER, it screamed in huge letters. A *small* piece, Dee's mom had said. I thought it would be tucked away behind the ads for old furniture and lost cats, not so big that only someone in a blindfold could possibly miss it.

I scanned the article. Sentences and quotes leaped out at me: "This young girl's unique gift…selflessly desperate to help the horses of this world…she hears their cries for help when no one else will listen…'Pia's gift snatched my valuable show pony from the jaws of certain death'…'Only Pia understood that my pony was a talented jumper'…'My pony was trapped in noseband hell until Pia heard her cries'"…and on it went. On and on. And on and *on*. Just like I'd said. Only worse. Much worse. Caroline Simpson had exaggerated my words. What had I been thinking?

I went all hot. Mom was going to kill me. But really, I had no one to blame but myself. I'd laid it on so thick, and Caroline Simpson had just written what I'd told her. How stupid was I? How was I going to explain this to Mom? Even so, I couldn't help a sneaky, private grin—I was certainly a celebrity. Wow! How annoyed was Cat going to be?

Mom didn't kill me, but she wasn't very pleased.

"Why are you making up such stories, Pia? I knew this would happen, typical broken home behavior. It's classic attention seeking. It's all your father's fault."

"It's not," I cried. "I'm not attention seeking and, well, actually, Mom, I *can* hear horses. I don't know how," I lied, "but I can. How else would I have known all those things about the ponies at the yard?"

"But how long has this been happening?" Mom asked.

"Only since we moved here." That was true. I hated twisting the truth to Mom, but I didn't dare tell her about Epona. She might have wanted me to give her to a museum or something. I couldn't risk it; she was my key to celebrity status. Without Epona I was just the geeky new girl at the yard and at school. I was just starting to make friends in this new, unwanted life of ours. And without her, I wouldn't be able to talk to Drummer. I had to keep Epona; she was my lucky charm.

"Why didn't you tell me?" Mom asked. She looked truly hurt. We argued back and forth for a bit more, and I managed to persuade her that I could really hear the ponies, that I wasn't making it up or going crazy. But Mom didn't seem mad about that—it was the fact that I'd kept it a secret, that I hadn't confided in her.

"I'm really sorry," I said. And I was. I didn't realize she would be so upset about it. "I wish I had told you—but I'm not sure you believe me, even now."

"Mmmm, I'm not sure myself. It's a lot to take in," Mom said. "Well, why not?" she continued sniffily. "If your dad can run off with a woman half my age and weight, why shouldn't you be able to talk to horses?"

"Mom, don't," I pleaded. I hadn't heard her say anything bitter about Dad since we'd moved out of our old home. I thought she was getting better about him and Skinny Lynny and starting to move on. And I felt a little guilty. Since the Epona thing, I hadn't given much thought to how Mom was coping, and even less thought about Dad and Skinny Lynny. It had been a relief really. I'd thought about nothing else for so long. My dad and his horrible new girlfriend had dominated my thoughts and had been the cause of our upheaval. Now I realized that I'd never have heard Drummer and his friends if we hadn't moved here. I gave Mom a hug.

"I'm really sorry I didn't tell you. I'm glad you know now," I said.

"Anyway," added Mom, taking a deep breath, "I have something to tell you, too."

"Oh?" I asked. "What?"

"I'm going on a date this weekend."

I didn't know what to say. Talk about bombshell.

"Who with?" I finally managed to squeak.

"A very interesting man."

Interesting. I didn't like the sound of that. "Where did you meet him?" I felt like I was the parent, asking all these questions.

"He's a member of a club—we both are…"

"Not that stupid Internet dating club Carol belongs to?" I wailed, totally losing it.

"Mmmaaaaybeeeeee…"

"He'll be a psycho," I blurted out, "or he'll still be married. Or he'll breed rats, like the weirdo Carol dated from that very same club—the one who was totally bald at the front, with a ponytail at the back. The one with the gross tattoo."

"You're overreacting," Mom said, looking crestfallen. "And you're being very judgmental about people— that man with the ponytail was the nicest of all Carol's men friends. Don't forget, you said you would support me in this, Pia. It's difficult enough without you making it harder."

I had said I'd support her. *Why* had I said that? She had me backed into a corner anyway, because of the newspaper feature—and she had been good about it; she could have been a lot worse. I couldn't make a fuss about her date, could I? I smiled. I tried extra hard to make it look sincere— not sure whether I pulled it off.

"OK. I hope you have a great time," I said, giving her another hug. "But *please* don't tell me all about it," I pleaded. We both giggled together and everything was almost how it had been before Carol had told on me.

"Can I go and see Drummer now?" I said.

"Of course. And get something to eat on your way home. I'll give you the money," Mom said, fetching her purse. Things were all right again.

When I got to the yard, all the stables were empty and the ponies were in the field. Friday night—perhaps everyone was out partying, I thought. I didn't feel like riding. I could ride tomorrow—Drum could have a night off. Besides, I figured he was hungry. So I grabbed Drum's halter—I'd just check him over and give him his feed.

Once he knew we weren't going riding, Drum wanted to come in and I checked him for cuts and scratches, and then lifted his feet in turn to check his shoes.

"I think my off fore is a bit loose," Drum said, screwing up one eye as he carefully scratched his nose on the door frame, leaving red hairs on the wood. "Where's this feed you promised?"

"I don't know why I'm taking the trouble to give you the once-over, when you can just tell me if anything's amiss," I grumbled.

"Good idea," agreed Drum. "I'll just yell from the field next time. Save you the trouble of getting me in and going riding," he said.

"Nice try!" I cried, waving a fly away. "You're not getting out of work that easily!"

We both heard the clip-clop of hooves and my heart skipped a beat when I saw James and Moth walking along the drive. Moth was walking at a hundred miles an hour, as usual, and James sat tall in the saddle, his feet dangling

88

below the stirrups, his reins in loops. He still wore clothes that looked like they'd come from charity shops, but he somehow managed to look pretty good in them, scruffy though they were. How come my heart was doing somersaults when I harbored such nasty thoughts about James and his pony? I mean, I couldn't possibly think he was hot if he mistreated Moth. I busied myself getting Drum's feed and tipping it into his stall as James opened his stable door and let Moth walk in by herself, following behind.

"Had a good ride?" I asked, ultracasually, leaning over his half door.

"Hi!" greeted James, taking off his riding hat and running his hands through his hair, which made it stick up in a gorgeous, knee-melting kind of way. "Yes, thanks. We did all the jumps in the wood before paddling in the river to cool off."

I watched Moth as James untacked her, anxious for any clues about their relationship. Would she shy away from him as she had from me?

"How is Drummer settling in?" asked James, rubbing Moth's back where the saddle had been to encourage the circulation to return. Moth stood like a rock, her head high, her eyes toward me. It looked to me like she stood a little too rigidly. Could she be scared to move?

"Really good, thanks," I replied. "He seems to have made some friends."

"That's good. Most of the ponies get OK here," James told me, walking toward the door. Moth stayed where she was until James left the stable. Then she ventured forward to stand just inside the door, glancing at us. Most ponies I know shove and push you out of the way in a friendly manner. Moth was politeness personified, unlike...

"Finished! Let me out!" Drummer called from his stable next door.

"I'm going to turn Drum out again," I explained to James.

"Wait for me. Moth's going out, too," said James. "I'll just dump her tack."

We walked to the field together. Drummer kept pushing me in the small of my back to make me hurry up—he thinks it's funny—but Moth had much better manners, walking beside James and looking straight ahead. It was almost like...like...I struggled to find the words. Like she was trying to be invisible so that no one would notice her.

Inside the field gate Drummer frisked me for treats (which he found, of course) and then trotted off to find Bluey, his new best friend. He did a detour toward Bambi, but Catriona's skewbald mare flattened her ears along the back of her neck and bared her teeth at him. She plainly wasn't going to be worn down by his advances. Moth accepted James's treat and then stood with her ears moving in all directions, clearly agitated. Stroking her face, James slipped off the halter, watching Moth turn on her haunches and canter off. To me, it looked as though she couldn't wait to get away from James. And still I hadn't heard her say anything. Not a word. I could hear the others talking to one another. I heard Bambi be very rude to Drum as he tried his luck, heard him tell her to keep her mane on, heard Bluey welcome his friend back, heard Tiffany tell Bambi she was going over to the water trough for a drink and did she want to come, but Moth stayed as silent as the grave.

James and I wandered back to the yard and said our nights. Then I pedaled to the local diner. There was a long line. (Of course, Friday! The *worst* day to get a burger from the diner!) So I stood in line thinking about Moth. She hadn't seemed exactly *scared* of James. She'd seemed sort of...well, sort of *wary*. She'd been much better with James than she had with me. But then I'd once read something somewhere about how people who are abused or unkindly treated were often nice to their abusers because they were scared of upsetting them and getting more abuse. Could that be the case with Moth? How could James seem so nice if he was nasty to his pony—I mean, Cat I could understand! Thoughts churned around and around in my mind before the woman behind me asked me whether I could wake up. Apparently, I'd ignored the man asking for my order three times.

When I got to the yard the next day, someone had pinned up the article from the *Herald* in the feed room, so everyone had seen it. Bean and Katy were excited about being quoted; James gave me a wink (which made my knees wobble—I'm that pathetic!) as he rode out of the yard on Moth. Even Mrs. Collins said she'd seen the article, although she said she wasn't sure about "this horse whispering stuff."

Oh, and I met Mrs. Bradley, who was grooming her black Dales pony, Henry, with a dandy brush, under the pretense of grooming. Henry was tied up outside his stable on far too long a rope. It was the perfect length if Henry liked skipping, but not so successful as a means of keeping him in one place.

Mrs. Bradley nabbed me as I walked past on my way to the barn and asked me whether I could hear dear Henry saying anything. I could, but I decided that repeating "Get this stupid woman away from me; I'm fed up with her tickling me with the brush" wasn't very tactful. Instead, I told Mrs. B that Henry thought the world of her, and her face lit up like a Christmas tree. Phew!

Drum and I went riding with Katy and Bluey again, and we had a great time exploring farther afield. Even Drummer agreed it had been a great ride, and as we found some jumps for Bluey to tackle, he was happy, too.

Then, when I got home, things took a downward turn.

Carol was there, helping Mom with her makeover for her hot date, as Carol was calling it. Mom looked a little sick and nervous—Carol had bullied her into having new highlights—and they'd been out shopping for clothes and makeup. Honestly, talk about a couple of giggling girlies! I thought grown-ups were supposed to act, well, grown up. Mom was sitting there with a towel around her shoulders and looking all oven ready with tin foil in her hair, and the back of Carol's hand looked like a paint chip sampling card, smothered with lipstick splotches for Mom to choose her perfect color from.

"So you'll call me at eight thirty, just in case I want out?" Mom said to Carol.

"Of course! If he's awful, you can make an excuse and leave, say it's an emergency," Carol replied, applying too much blush to Mom's cheeks.

"It's only a drink at the local bar," Mom continued. "I'll be home by eleven, Pia."

"If she isn't, Pia, you call me!" said Carol. She is so bossy.

"I've got too much makeup on," Mom said, looking in the mirror. "Take some off, Carol. I look like I'm trying too hard."

"You don't have to try too hard, Suze; you're gorgeous!" squawked Carol. "Now let's get your new outfit on!"

"What do you think, Pia?" asked Mom.

They'd teamed a new blue dress with Mom's short jacket and she had some high heels on, too. Actually, she looked pretty gorgeous—I mean, for someone her age. I hadn't noticed under Mom's usual casual clothes just how much weight she'd lost, but she looked really slim and much younger than usual. Having her hair styled made a difference; usually she just wore it tied back.

"You look sensational!" I said. And I meant it. I felt a bit strange about it, actually. I mean, here was my mom, looking glamorous, geared up for a date with a strange man who wasn't my dad. It made me gulp a bit.

They giggled and preened and giggled some more until I couldn't stand it, so after enthusiastically wishing Mom a great time on her date (I'm not a bad actress), I fled up to the stables again, even though Drummer was out in the field and technically enjoying Drummer time.

I found him grazing with Bluey.

"What's up?" he said. "You look a little down-in-the-dumps."

I suddenly felt very miserable. I hadn't been expecting Drummer to notice anything. It suddenly hit me; my mom was moving on. Dating a new man. What if she liked him? What if she *married* him?

"You wouldn't understand, Drum," I said, leaning against his warm, dark neck. I didn't want to cry, but two renegade tears plopped onto Drummer's coat and glistened in the low evening sun. I had always confided in Drummer whenever things had got tough. I'd told him about Dad, about Skinny Lynny, about us having to move. He'd always been my sounding board. This was the first time, though, it was a two-way thing.

"Things at home changing again?" said Drum, nuzzling me. I put my arms around his neck and howled. I felt so confused; I wanted Mom to be happy, but I was scared, too. Everything was changing so fast. I told Drum how I felt and my fears about Mom.

"Well, we can't stop change," he said. "I didn't want to come here—I miss my friends back at the old yard, but I've made some new ones. Bluey's a good friend, and I'll wear Bambi down in the end, you see if I don't. Just because things change, it doesn't mean they have to change for the worse. It rather depends on how you tackle it. Come on, buck up—you've still got me!"

"Oh, Drummer," I sniffed, "you are a nice pony, after all."

"What do you mean, *after all?* I'm the Drummer, the best!" Drum replied. "Now stop crying; you're making my coat all wet."

"Why can't you be nice like this all the time?" I said, wiping my eyes on my sleeve.

"You must be joking! Far too much of a strain. I have my reputation to think of. Now run along and grow up!" Drum replied. But he said it kindly, nudging me gently with his nose.

"I can't wait to be a grown-up," I said. "Everything will be easy then."

"You couldn't be more wrong," Drum replied. "No one *ever* grows up. Just ask your mom."

"Your human is such a crybaby!" It was Bambi, wandering past. She sounded like Catriona and for a split second I was terrified she would tell Catriona I'd been crying. Then I remembered that she couldn't.

Drummer lifted his head. "Get lost, you nosy old mare!" he yelled.

Time stood still as every pony head jerked upward, and I heard a loud, collective equine gasp. The silence that followed was so thick, you could have sliced it with a shovel.

Bambi's eyes glinted and she gave Drummer a look that made me shiver. Drummer lifted his head defiantly.

"Come on, Bambi," said Tiffany. "Take no notice of him; he's just a weirdo." And they walked indignantly to the far side of the field, as far away as they could get from Drummer, their tails swishing defiantly.

"Now you've done it!" whispered Bluey. "Bambi's very sensitive about her looks."

"What do you mean? I never said anything about her looks," Drum retorted.

"Yeah, but you called her old!" Bluey explained. "She'll never forgive you. Never, *ever!*"

"She will," Drummer said. "It'll do her good to learn I'm no pushover. She was getting a little full of herself."

"You stood up for me," I said, kissing Drum's furry, black nose. "You're the best pony in the world."

"Don't you forget it!" said Drummer, gruffly. "Got any sweets?" he added, nuzzling my pockets.

I sneaked back to get my bike. I didn't want anyone to see I'd been crying—I'd already caused Drum enough trouble with Bambi.

The house was eerily empty when I got home. After making myself a cheese omelet, I switched on the TV and trawled through the channels watching bits of everything, and then my cell phone rang. My heart leaped.

I bet that's Mom, I thought. I bet she's coming home early because her date's so awful.

But it wasn't Mom.

At first I thought it was a joke, that someone was punking me, but by the time the call ended, I realized that I was *so* a horsey celebrity and I could do nothing but leap about the house and whoop with excitement. Because the call was from a TV channel and they wanted me, Pia, the Pony Whisperer, as billed in the *Bretstone*

Herald, to appear on Cecily Armstrong's early evening talk show next week.

I was going to be on TV! Racing upstairs, I pulled Epona out of my pocket and planted a big kiss on where her nose should have been. I was so excited, I thought I might explode!

CHAPTER 8

I SAT IN THE ROOM everyone had been ushered into prior to filming—and felt a bit sick. TV—scary! Mom was drinking the complimentary wine—we'd come on the train—and she was starting to laugh a bit too loudly with the other people in the room with us—a man who was promoting his new book about frogs, another man who was introduced to us as one of the other horse experts (I'm an expert! I thought, amazed), and a woman called Kelly from the show who was looking after us.

"So your daughter hears horses, eh?" said the *other* horse expert. He was very stylish and was matching Mom glass for glass in wine.

"Yes," said Mom, nodding furiously and waving her glass about. "Yes, she does." At least she believed me now. Or perhaps it suited her to believe me.

"How unusual," he remarked, clearly *not* believing it.

"It's simply amazing!" Mom replied. I cringed.

The door opened and in came someone who looked familiar. A man, not very tall, and a bit older than Mom. He was dressed in a black shirt and black trousers, and his hair was starting to go gray. My stomach took a turn around the block as I realized who it was—Alex Willard, horse behaviorist extraordinaire! I was going to be on TV with Alex Willard. How cool was that?

But first, Alex Willard had to run the gauntlet with my mom.

"Hello," Mom said, smiling. "Are you a horse expert?" Talk about cringe, I mean, who doesn't know Alex Willard? It would be like asking Father Christmas whether he worked on Christmas Eve.

"I suppose you could say that, yes," Alex replied, smiling.

"What do you do?" asked Mom. Then she narrowed her eyes, looking at Alex Willard intently. "No, don't tell me...let me guess..."

Just when I thought it couldn't get worse...

"A racehorse trainer? A show jumper? One of those people who fits shoes to horse's feet—what are they called, Pia?"

"I'm a horse behaviorist." Alex put us both out of our misery. He spoke softly, like you would to a nervous pony or a dog.

"Are you married?" asked Mom. I could have died. Right there. Forget fame and fortune, forget celebrity. My mom was drinking too much and actually flirting. In front of me. With Alex Willard. *Gross!*

"Er, no," said Alex Willard, a bit taken aback.

"Mom, please!" I hissed.

"I'm Sue Edwards, pleased to meet you," Mom said, extending her hand.

"Alex Willard," said Alex Willard. He didn't add that he was *the* celebrated behaviorist who gave clinics and had broken in thousands of horses with his revolutionary methods. I gulped. I was going to be on TV with Alex Willard. Wow!

"I'm divorced," Mom said, not quite slurring her words. "Pia here is my only child." She put her arm around my shoulders and squeezed. "My baby girl!"

"You must be very proud of her," Alex Willard said kindly, grinning at me.

"I am, I am, you couldn't be more right. I am *proud* of my Pia," Mom rambled. I could have gone through the floor.

Suddenly, a woman about Mom's age arrived. She was all breathless, peeling off her coat and smoothing her jet-black hair.

"I am *sooooo* sorry I'm late. The traffic! I'd have been *mortified* if I'd missed it. Oh, Alex, hello, how lovely to see you!"

"Emma, darling. You look wonderful," replied Alex Willard, and they exchanged air kisses.

"Oh, and Jeremy's here, too. I didn't know they'd asked you. How splendid! I was so sure you were going to win at the Badminton horse trials. Such bad luck falling off over the last."

I gulped again, taking another look at the expert who was already there, the one who didn't believe me. Jeremy Lampeter, three-day eventer. How come he looked so different in real life without his riding hat on? I suddenly wondered how I was going to look on TV. Would anyone recognize me in the street afterward? How could I be a celebrity if no one recognized me?

Then Emma, whoever she was, turned to me.

"And you must be *the Pony Whisperer!*" she gushed, pounding toward me.

"I'm Pia's mother, Sue Edwards," interjected Mom, planting herself between the woman and me. Thank goodness—I was sure her lips were going to suck all the air from around me, too.

"Emma Ellison, horse healer. You've probably heard of me."

I hadn't. It seemed rude to admit it so I just smiled.

"What, like a vet?" asked Mom.

"No, no, bless you," said Emma Ellison, helping herself to a large glass of white wine. "I feel horses' pain, I heal them—either by laying on of hands or from a distance—I can do both. It's very rewarding work—not unlike what your daughter does—I was sent a clipping about you in your local newspaper by a fan. Told me I had some competition, ha, ha." Her voice shot upward—it could have shattered glass. Lowering it to a less jarring level, she whispered, "But, seriously, the young can be very in tune with the suffering of animals. If it isn't nurtured and encouraged, it is lost. So sad." Emma Ellison stared at me intently. "I can sense that you have the gift, too. Yes, yes, you're one of us, young Pia!"

So much for *her* gift, I thought!

Another woman from the TV show came into the room. "Two minutes." She smiled. "We'll get you settled on the sofas while we go for a commercial break."

101

"Good luck, baby!" whispered Mom, kissing me on the cheek and splashing wine on my black jeans.

"Mom!" She'd been a bit clingy since her hot date on Saturday night. It had been OK, she'd said. He'd been very nice, her date Gary; he worked in insurance. Might see him again, might not. I wondered whether the decision was to be hers or Gary's. It didn't sound as though she was going to marry the guy, so I'd relaxed a bit.

Anyway, the TV invite had been so exciting (Carol was a little put out. Ha!) that we'd spoken of little else all week. Mom had cleared it with the school for me to take an afternoon off, and Drummer had been unimpressed. Not surprisingly as he doesn't get to watch a lot of TV.

"So explain it to me again," he'd said, only half paying attention because he was chewing a carrot I'd brought him.

"It means thousands, even millions of people can see me—it's a box that beams pictures of me into people's homes. Like, if there was one in the stable here, you could see me in the studio, talking to the woman whose show it is, Cecily Armstrong. It's the Cecily Armstrong show. It's made in the afternoon."

"So who watches it, then?" Drummer had asked. "Isn't everyone at school or at work?"

"It's shot in the afternoon, but broadcast later, in the early evening," I'd told him. I didn't go into the intricacies of TV.

"Shot? Now what are you talking about?"

"Never mind."

"Can I come?"

"Not really. It's in the city. In a studio. I can't really picture you riding on the subway."

"What's a subway?"

"I wish you could come," I'd said. "I'm a bit scared."

"Don't worry," mumbled Drummer, giving himself a shake so that dust flew out of his coat and wafted onto me. "I'll be thinking of you. Just remember that."

I was remembering as my microphone was being fitted to my sweater. Taking a deep breath, I sent out thoughts to Drummer. "I know you're thinking of me, Drummer," I heard my voice in my head. "I'm going to need all your help in the next ten minutes." It sounds crazy, but it helped. I could see in my mind Drummer standing by the field gate, concentrating on me and sending positive thoughts back. What a great pony he was! And maybe I was one of Emma Ellison's tribe, after all; I could see Drummer so clearly in my mind. Maybe I really was psychic!

We settled ourselves on the sofas opposite Cecily Armstrong. Blond, with makeup, and smartly dressed, she smiled warmly at everyone and winked at me. Jeremy and Alex sat on one sofa, leaving me to share the other with Emma Ellison. Patting my arm, Emma leaned toward me, her mouth splitting her face in two as she beamed. She looked demented.

"I can feel you're nervous, but don't worry, I'm here," she told me.

She was right; I had been nervous. Now I was downright scared!

The commercial break over, someone counted Cecily down and she turned to the camera, telling it that she had been joined by some extraordinary people from the world of horses. Alex Willard, the celebrated horse behaviorist; Emma Ellison, an animal healer; Jeremy Lampeter, the famous three-day eventer; and young Pia Edwards, the Pony Whisperer, an extraordinary young woman who had recently discovered that she could actually hear what horses and ponies were saying.

Wow, I thought, I really am a celebrity!

"So starting with you, Alex, if I may," Cecily continued; "what do you say to anyone who says that horses don't have the same feelings or thoughts as we do?"

Alex Willard gently argued that he believed that horses did possess feelings—and Emma Ellison butted in with her own views, largely based on some of her more famous clients, racehorses, show jumpers, and the like. In the end, Cecily had to shut her up by bringing in someone else. That someone else was me.

"So, Pia, you can actually *hear* what the ponies are saying to you. Can you tell us a little more about that?" asked Cecily Armstrong, leaning forward intently.

"Yes," I said. My throat seemed to have closed up. I could see the studio audience out of the corner of my eye, see the cameras whizzing back and forth across the floor, the technicians with them. The lights were a bit hot. I wished Drum had been able to come—I'd have loved to hear what he would have said about it all.

"And I understand you've helped a number of ponies at the stables where you keep your pony. Drummer, isn't it?"

"Yes, Drummer is my pony. He's a wonderful bay with a white blaze, and I used to think I knew what he was thinking, but now that I can hear him talk to me, he's quite a different character." I was off—I can talk about Drummer all day.

"So tell us more about the ponies you've helped," prompted Cecily. So I did. I told her about Dolly and Tiffany and Bluey. Cecily wanted to know how I could hear the ponies, and I told her I didn't understand how, it just happened. Unexplainable, I said, shrugging my shoulders. I couldn't tell anyone about Epona. Not now.

Jeremy Lampeter butted in. "How do you know they're not just voices in your own head? I mean, honestly, hearing horses talking—come on!"

"You're not in tune; you won't open your heart," cried Emma Ellison, clutching dramatically at her own chest. "The horses talk to me, too—they tell me about their lives, their fears, their loves. You can't hear them because you've blocked them out. We all have the gift, but we choose not to use it." She looked as though she was about to cry.

"So what exactly do they say?" asked Jeremy, looking at me. "Come on, Pony Whisperer girl, do the Scottish Highland ponies talk with a Scots accent?"

"Actually, I hadn't thought of that—" I started.

"No, exactly!" interrupted Jeremy, sitting back and folding his arms.

"But now that you come to mention it…there's a Dales pony at the yard, and he talks with an East Coast accent. And Bluey's got an accent, too, but I don't know what it is. I'll ask him where he comes from."

Alex Willard threw back his head and laughed. "She's got you there, Jeremy!" he chuckled.

"I myself have more of a telepathic link with the horses; I *feel* what they say," said Emma Ellison, anxious to be back in the limelight.

"Well, I definitely hear the ponies—they're a bit like people, too," I continued, warming up. "They have their own friends and their enemies. Their feelings can be hurt. There's a skewbald pony at our yard who got very upset when Drummer called her a nosy old mare."

Alex Willard gave me a strange look. "Are you saying ponies can feel *insulted?*" he asked.

"Well, yes."

"You'll be telling us they enjoy a joke or two or revel in sarcasm next," said Jeremy. I was glad he'd fallen off at Badminton. I hoped he'd fall off again next year.

"Drummer is very sarcastic," I said, "but he does make me laugh, too."

"Horses are horses; they don't have feelings like we do," Jeremy snarled. "My horses just eat and sleep—and that's all."

"Well, Jeremy," began Alex Willard, "a lot of people would agree with you. But my studies show that each horse has its own personality, and horses communicate with each other— especially in the wild where their survival depends on it."

"Yes, of course, but that's a long way from being able to talk," snarled Jeremy.

"Perhaps you're not listening," said Emma Ellison, triumphantly. "If you listen, you can hear the horses reaching out to you; you can tune into their pain. I once helped a show jumper who had been a Spanish bullfighting horse in a previous life. With my help and understanding he was able to move on, become a very happy horse. He was stuck in the past, you see."

I decided that our horse healer friend was a bit of a nut and wondered whether I came across like her. I made a note to tone it down a bit, not so much of the hands-on trembling stuff so I didn't seem like a fruitcake, which was what Jeremy had me labeled as. And then I realized that I was doing the same thing to Emma Ellison—judging her. Perhaps she could really tune into horses. Perhaps she had her own Epona stashed away. I looked at her again. Or maybe she was just a *little* bit crazy.

"You know," I said, "Drummer is really interested in food. It's his favorite subject to talk about. Sometimes, I know he's only half listening to me because he's so preoccupied with eating." I was aware of Alex Willard staring at me again.

"Fascinating!" Cecily breathed, turning to the camera. "Well, that's remarkable, it really is and it's been so very interesting hearing all your views. I suppose we'll never really know, will we? We're going to take a short break now, but don't go away because after the break we'll be talking to a man about his obsession with frogs and asking the question, did a humble cabbage cause the downfall of the Roman Empire? See you soon!"

And that was it. The music went for the next commercial break and we were all hurried back into the room next to the studio, where the next guests waited nervously. Mom had trapped another poor man in the corner by the water dispenser.

"…so she's got him now, my husband, the father of my baby girl," she was saying.

"Well, you know, lots of men go through it as well," the man mumbled. His face lit up when he saw us all coming to rescue him.

"Of course they do, of course they do," agreed Mom, nodding furiously. "Let me give you my number. If you ever want to go out for a drink or something…" she added, fishing in her bag for a pen and a piece of paper.

"Mom, are you OK?" I said, gingerly.

"Oh, hello, sweetie. You were wonderful—I saw everything. Weren't you fantastic? You told that annoying, stuck-up man. Did you enjoy it?"

"Yes, it was exciting! Can we go now?"

"What? Oh, OK. I'll get my jacket."

I asked Alex Willard for his autograph.

"Of course, let me have your address and I'll send you my latest book if you like," he said.

"Oh, would you? That would be great! Everyone at the yard thinks you're fantastic!"

"Thank you, Pia. I think you're a pretty fantastic girl

yourself. I wish we could talk some more. Here's my number." He pulled out a card and gave it to me.

I was speechless, unfortunately. Just when I needed my voice to drown her out, Mom zoomed back.

"Ah, Mrs. Edwards, I hope you don't mind; I've just given Pia my card. Is that all right?"

"Oh, of course. That's very kind of you," said Mom, leaning a little bit too close to Alex Willard for comfort. "I understand—and do call me Sue," she whispered.

I couldn't leave fast enough.

"What did you mean, *you understand?*" I asked her as we walked to the underground station.

"Oh, he obviously wants me to call him," said Mom.

I wanted to scream. What was happening to my mom? She was after everything in pants. I could have killed Carol and her wretched makeover. It was pointless trying to tell her Alex wasn't interested in her. I decided to keep the card hidden—I'd tell her I'd lost it if she asked.

We got home about five, so I had time to run up and see Drummer before the show was aired. He was dozing by himself under a tree, the other ponies scattered about the field around him.

"Hey, you!" I said.

"Oh, you made me jump, sneaking up on me like that!" scolded Drummer, stretching a hind leg out behind him and grunting.

"I didn't sneak," I said. "In fact, I've been calling you since I got to the gate."

"What have you brought me? Apples? Carrots? Sugar lumps?"

"Have an apple," I offered. He took it delicately and chomped it all up.

"You're welcome," I said, pointedly.

"What? Oh, yeah, thanks. Actually, I think there was a worm in that one."

"So I went to the television studio today, to film the show. It's on tonight," I told Drummer. "It was much more difficult than I'd imagined, but it really helped to know you were thinking of me, sending me positive thoughts, so thanks. You're a pal."

"Was that TV thingamajig today?" said Drummer. My heart sank.

"You said you were going to send me some positive thoughts to get me through it. You promised," I ranted.

"Oh, well, you did get through it, didn't you? I mean, you didn't need me, did you?" Drummer said. He was completely unrepentant. Some pal.

"Are we going riding?" he asked. "Say no because I'm nice and relaxed out here. Though if you could splash around some of that super-duper fly repellent, I'd be grateful 'cause they seem to be on the warpath today."

"I've got it here," I told him. "Brace yourself."

I squirted, Drum shuddered, and the flies zoomed off to torment some other poor pony.

"Can't ride. I want to whiz home and see myself on TV," I told Drummer. "Oh, that sounds so weird!"

"Run off then. See you tomorrow. Have a nice time, you big-time celebrity," said Drummer, closing his eyes again.

I planted a kiss on his neck, got a taste of fly repellent for my trouble, which I spat out, and zoomed off home with mounting excitement. Mom had sobered up by the time I'd got back and was looking a bit sheepish.

"I wasn't tipsy, was I?" she asked me.

"Yes! You flirted with Alex Willard, the most famous horse behaviorist in the world, and you asked for some man's number and asked him on a date."

"Oh. Well. So what?" Mom said, defensively. She went a bit pink, though.

We set the DVR, of course. This was one for posterity! As the show before Cecily Armstrong's finished and the commercials took over, I felt really nervous and excited. This was the start of my celebrity career.

The titles rolled, the recorder kicked into life, and there I was with Alex Willard and horrible Jeremy and batty Emma, and my voice didn't sound like mine, and I was fidgeting and I looked tiny on the sofa next to Emma. Mom and I squealed all the way through and bounced up and down on our own sofa with excitement.

And then it was all over.

"Wow!" gasped Mom. "How thrilling was that?"

We played it again—and Carol called Mom on her cell phone in the middle of it and Mom giggled a lot before hanging up. Then my cell phone rang and it was Katy and she was all excited—especially about Alex Willard and she

111

wanted to know all about it—and Mom went off to make herself a coffee and I was about to play the DVR once more when my phone rang yet again.

"Hello!" I said.

"Hello, is that Pia?"

"Yes." Pia, the Pony Whisperer, I wanted to add, but didn't.

"Pia! We were both so excited to see you on the television—and surprised, of course. Why didn't you tell us you were going to be on the Cecily Armstrong show? We could have come along with you!"

For a split second I was perplexed. I couldn't place the voice—and then when I realized who it was, I caught my breath and hastily glanced toward the kitchen to see whether Mom could see me.

The voice belonged to Skinny Lynny.

CHAPTER 9

O**H, ER, HELLO, S**KIN...I mean, Lyn," I spluttered. What did she want? She never calls me. *Ever*—thank goodness!

"How exciting for you," she continued in her wispy, faux little girl voice. I wanted to slap her—a little tricky on the phone, though.

"And what's this about you claiming to be able to talk to horses? Paul said he didn't know anything about it. He's quite upset you didn't confide in him," Skinny Lynny went on to scold me. Rude! Calls me up and tells me off. She was the worst, snotty witch.

"Can I speak to Dad, please?" I said, ever so politely.

"Of course, I'll get him...Paul!"

"Hi, Pumpkin!" It was Dad. "What's all this about you being a pony whisperer? First I've heard about it. Weren't you going to tell your old dad?"

"Of course I was. It's just that everything happened so quickly," I mumbled.

"So you're hearing Drummer these days, then?" he laughed.

"I can, Dad. I really can hear what the ponies are saying, including Drummer." I didn't blame anyone for not believing me.

"Well, you've always been so nutty about horses, I always said you'd turn into one, didn't I? Remember?" Dad joked. "What does your mom think about it all, then?"

I glanced across at Mom. She'd come out of the kitchen and was looking at me in a strange way. She knew it was Dad on the phone.

"She's fine about it. Look, I was in the local paper, too. I'll send you a copy of the article if you like," I offered.

"You do that, sweetheart. You mustn't forget your old dad now that you're famous. Are you OK? Need anything?"

"No, thanks, Dad. And thanks for paying for Drummer's keep. He's still the best."

"No problem. You must come and stay with me and Lyn soon. Lyn keeps saying so."

I bet she doesn't, I thought.

"Maybe next month?" Dad said. I *so* didn't want to. Stuck without Drummer, having to watch my dad being schmoozed by Skinny Lynny? I didn't think so.

"Sure," I said, not meaning it.

"And if you're going to be on the television again, let us know. We might have missed it. I can't let my only daughter be a TV star without seeing her, can I?"

"Of course," I mumbled. "I'm really sorry. I'll let you know if there's a next time."

Mom was a bit brittle for a while after the phone call, but we watched me on the DVR again, and that cheered us both up.

The next morning, I was plunged into full-blown,

114

top-of-the-range celebrity status. It started the moment I got to the school gates.

"Hey, it's the Pony Whisperer!" someone shouted. Almost everyone around me turned in my direction. A girl from the year above me, a kind of a tough girl, took a step forward and looked me up and down. Uh-oh, I thought, there's a distinct danger of me getting roughed up here.

"I saw you on TV," she said, her face breaking into a smile. "Cool!"

"Can I have your autograph?" asked another of the girls. Then all hell broke loose:

"What was it like being on TV?"

"Did you see anyone famous?"

"Are you going to be on TV again?"

"Will you get your own show?"

"Hey, *Tia*, you big fat liar!"

Catriona had arrived—just when it was going so well, too. Her short hair was styled so that it stuck out in a chic way and she had a lacy blouse on instead of a school shirt— strictly against the rules. She looked just how I would love to look—sort of edgy and rebellious. My heart sank, but today, I had some allies.

"She's been on TV, so she can't be lying," said someone. A little trusting of them, I thought. Little did *they* know.

"And what's that other lie you told about Bambi being insulted? Your useless old nag couldn't insult Bambi if he tried. She's way superior to him."

"You watched it, then?" I couldn't resist saying.

"Only because I couldn't believe you were going to keep up this ridiculous charade," Cat replied. Her emerald eyes glared at me with pure hatred. She was extremely mad.

"Alex Willard didn't seem to think I was lying—he gave me his number and told me to call him sometime," I told her, rubbing it in. Catriona turned pink. I wondered whether she was going to burst. Then I wondered what would happen if she did burst—would we all be splattered with bits of Catriona?

"Another lie!" she spat out. "Alex Willard is much too important to bother with *you*. You're just making it up."

"I didn't make up being on the television," I said, turning and walking into school. Several of the other girls followed me, asking more questions, and by the time I got to my homeroom, my head was spinning. So this was being a celebrity—it was exhausting!

We all shuffled into assembly and I kept as far away from Catriona as possible. I was staring out of the hall window, wondering whether Katy would be up for a ride this evening, when I suddenly realize my name was being mentioned by Mr. Frencham, the ancient teacher up on the stage.

What have I done now? I thought, listening for once.

"…seems she has a remarkable talent and is so in tune with ponies, they can communicate with her. I cannot remember a time when a pupil of this school appeared on television, er, not in so positive a manner, anyway. Pia Edwards, where are you? Make yourself known."

I didn't have to. Everyone in my class turned to look at me—I stood out like a Chihuahua at a greyhound convention. So, of course, everyone else in the assembly craned their necks, turned around, or stood on tiptoe to see me, too. And it was my turn to go pink. This celebrity gig was getting to be kind of a pain.

"Pia, please be good enough to see me in my office after the assembly."

I gulped. Was I going to get a right old telling off? Catriona leaned forward and glanced in my direction.

"He knows you're lying!" she said. "And he's not the only one!"

Technically, Catriona was right because without Epona, I couldn't hear diddly-squat from any ponies. I wasn't so much a Pony Whisperer as a Pony Fraud. Oh, triple pooh, why had I let it get this far? I should have just shut up and kept it between Drummer and myself. But no, Pia, I told myself, you had to mouth off about it, didn't you? You dummy!

I chewed my nails like a starving woman. Mr. Frencham kept me waiting outside his office for what seemed like ages so I had progressed to my cuticles and my fingers by the time he finally called me in. Is it considered cannibalism if you eat yourself?

"Sit down, Pia," Mr. Frencham said, waving at a chair opposite his desk. I sat. I couldn't chomp on my hands anymore so I chewed the inside of my cheek instead. At this rate, I thought, I'll disappear down my own stomach.

That'll get me on TV again—on the news, *Pony Whisperer devours herself,* and…

"It isn't often one of the school's pupils is subjected to so much positive publicity," Mr. Frencham began, interrupting my thoughts.

"No, sir," I said, gulping down half of my own cheek.

"So I wanted to ask you, Pia, should you be asked to appear on any more chat shows or be featured in the press, whether you would be good enough to mention the school?"

My brain started to whirl. It does that when it's confused. It does it mainly during math and quite a lot in geography.

"Or even," Mr. Frencham continued, "wear the school uniform. It would be so very good for the school, you see, with funding and the like. What do you say?"

I wanted to say, "Get lost!" What nerve! Who wants to be seen on TV in their school uniform, for goodness' sake?

But instead, I said, "Er, well, sir, I'd like to…but…" I had to think fast. "But the TV company told me what they wanted me to wear."

Mr. Frencham looked crestfallen. "Oh, I see. Well, never mind."

I sped back to class. Then I wished I hadn't been in such a hurry because it was math. But Miss Ashad, the glam-looking math teacher who's a little celebrity-obsessed and always has copies of *People* and *US Weekly* magazines poking out of her mock designer bags, wanted me to tell her all about Cecily Armstrong and her TV show so that wasted a good ten minutes. My classmates chipped in with some questions of their own to keep it going for as long as possible and delay the start of the lesson—only Catriona sat mute, with a face like thunder. She didn't dare say anything in front of Miss Ashad.

I was pretty glad when the morning was over and we all trooped off to lunch. Mel and her friend Michelle grabbed me by my sleeves and insisted I go to lunch with them. It seemed I was the new friend of choice. It was a bit embarrassing. After all, they didn't really want to be with me; they just wanted to be with the Pony Whisperer, TV celebrity. However, having had enough of eating lunch by myself, I thought a couple of hanger-on false friends were not to be sniffed at. And they introduced me to some of *their* friends, who were also impressed by my celebrity status.

I started to feel uncomfortable about it. I mean, it's one thing thinking you'd like to be a celeb, but another when you feel everyone wants to talk to you only *because* you're celeb, not because of who you actually are. It seemed that all of a sudden I had no control over this pony whispering thing; it had taken control over me. And it had made Catriona hate me even more.

And just as I was half laughing at Mel's joke about a monkey and a trumpet, I noticed James sitting at a table across the dining hall, with his own—real—friends. And as I spotted him, he turned to me and winked, waving in my direction.

"Are you friends with James Beecham?" asked Mel.

119

"Yes," I said, waving back even though I knew I could never be friends with anyone who mistreated a pony. If *only* Moth would talk to me, I'd know whether my suspicions were right.

"Oooh, Cat thinks he's dishy," Mel giggled.

"She's not the only one," sighed one of her friends. "I think he's dreamy. He's just so good-looking—I'm thinking of staying behind to watch soccer just because he's on the team."

It seemed that everyone had the hots for James. But, I thought, he winked and waved at *me*. But then, was he winking at Pia or at the Pony Whisperer? I was getting paranoid. And anyway, I thought, what did I care whether James was winking at the real me or the celeb me? He had still winked at *me*. It still counted. If only there wasn't the Moth question. My mind raced ahead, bouncing around ideas I couldn't stop. Maybe James was scared Moth would talk to me, and he'd be *so* busted if she did. Could that be the reason behind his friendliness? Fear of being found out? Mel's voice dragged my concentration back to the dining hall.

"This is Scott. He's got a horse and he wants to meet you," she said.

Scott was tall and dark, a little dangerous looking, and at least three years older than me. I had no idea how Mel knew him but didn't really care.

"What's your horse called, Scott?" Mel continued.

"Warrior," said Scott. He smiled at me. "Maybe you could ride over to my yard one day and act as a go-between between him and me."

"Er, um, yes, if you like," I spluttered. This was so weird, suddenly being noticed by people—totally different from my first week at school when I was practically invisible. It felt so *weird!*

"I'll hold you to that," said Scott, and he was dragged away by his friends who couldn't understand why he was talking to a bunch of girls three years down.

"So would you actually be able to talk to Scott's horse, then?" asked one of Michelle's friends.

"Of course, she would. Haven't you been listening?" exclaimed Michelle.

"Oh, well, I didn't know whether she could just hear her own pony, and he told her what the others were saying," her friend mumbled, unaware that her words caused me to have an absolute *eureka* moment.

The realization that I was completely stupid hit me like a slap with a wet fish (and not for the first time, let me tell you!). I hadn't asked the one person who was in a unique position to find out about Moth and her iffy behavior. The one person who had inside knowledge, the one person I could trust not to say anything about it to *anyone.*

Drummer!

Why had I only just thought of it? Dim, extra dim, dim-squared, dim-with-dumb-on-top Pia. Some Pony Whisperer I was!

It was time to bring on Drummer Holmes, detective pony. Solving the Moth mystery was bound to be elementary for my dear Drummer!

CHAPTER 10

DRUMMER, IT SEEMED, DIDN'T want to play.

"The thing is, Drum," I told him as I tied him up outside his stable and got to work brushing him over with the dandy brush, "you're in a unique position to clear something up."

"Go easy with that around my tummy, please," Drummer said, wrinkling his nose up against the dust.

"I'm always very gentle, you know that."

"Mmmm, there's your idea of gentle, and there's *my* idea of gentle. They don't seem to bear any resemblance."

"Anyway, as I was saying," I continued, "I have this problem you can help me with."

"You're always whining about something," said Drum. "Just go with the flow for once and stop fussing."

"It's about Moth," I began. "I need to know whether James treats her well. You know, like I treat you. Or does he"—I stopped brushing and leaned toward Drummer's head, lowering my voice—"ill-treat her? I mean, she acts very strangely around people. Like she's wary of them. I really need to know because James is being nice to me and I don't know whether to be nice back or confront him with my suspicions. It's very awkward. Plus, of course, if he were being unkind to Moth, he needs to be stopped. You understand, don't you?"

Drummer screwed up his nose. Then his eyelashes twitched. He appeared to be thinking. Hard. Then he spoke.

"Can't help you," he snapped.

"What? What do you mean?" I asked. "Why can't you help me?"

"It's against the code."

"Code? What code?"

"The equine code. You wouldn't understand. It's a confidentiality thing we ponies have. I couldn't possibly tell you anything about Moth in that way, unless she asked me to. It wouldn't be ethical."

"What, not even if I could help? Not even if I could do something about it?" I said, amazed.

"Nope, sorry! Subject closed," snapped Drummer and stared into the distance.

"You're making this code thing up," I said irritably. "After all, how many people can you actually talk to? I'm about the only one so you can't have a code already in place. You're just being unhelpful."

Drum ignored me.

"I bet you don't know anything," I said, hoping to trick Drum into telling me. "I bet you're embarrassed that you know nothing about it and I've noticed. Huh!"

Drummer wasn't fooled. "I'm saying nothing!" he mumbled. And that, it seemed, was that. So much for my fabulous plan! So much for having someone on the inside, so to speak. I'd have to resort to plan B. If only I had a plan B!

As I groomed Drummer, other people began to arrive at the yard. Leanne sauntered out of her mom's very expensive-looking SUV. Katy waved at me as she went to the field to get Bluey so we could go riding together, and I watched Pippin being led across the yard to her stable very slowly by Bethany and her mom. The sun was out; the birds were singing. It was a perfect Saturday morning and I decided to take Drum's advice and stop worrying and whining. Today, I decided, I was just going to enjoy myself as I used to before Epona came into my life.

I was lifting Drum's saddle down from the rack when Leanne came into the tack room, all earrings, eye makeup, and fancy blue and brown clothes. She always looked like she'd spent ages selecting riding gear that matched perfectly.

"Er, hi, Pia. How's it going?" she said, hesitantly.

I smiled back. "Good, thanks," I said, hooking Drummer's bridle over the back of the saddle.

"Have you got a minute?" Leanne said. "I was just wondering…" she began, looking around. There was no one else there. "…whether you could maybe talk to Mr. Higgins, see if he has anything to say. You know, whether he wants to tell me anything. Would you mind just taking a moment to see?"

I was a little stunned. Then I realized why Leanne was looking so furtive—she was probably worried Catriona would see her talking to me. She wouldn't like it.

"Oh, yes, OK," I agreed. It wasn't Leanne's fault Cat hated me so why not? I put Drummer's tack back, followed

Leanne to Mr. Higgins's stable, and looked over the door. Even though it was the middle of summer, Mr. Higgins wore a light stable rug. When he went out in the field with the other ponies, Leanne made sure he had a light-weight turnout rug on, too. It kept his coat clean for her dressage shows. I'd never seen him looking anything but sparkling clean and tidy. His mane was pulled short, his tail trimmed to just below his hocks, and his heels clipped so that his black legs were smooth and slender. He looked like a miniature racehorse.

"I just wondered if he was OK, whether there was any-thing he wanted to say to me," Leanne explained, her earrings glinting in the sunlight. Nothing unusual there. Who wouldn't want to know what their pony was thinking?

Nervously, I felt for Epona in my pocket. She was there, nestled in the corner, collecting the fluff that seems to grow in pockets. I hoped Mr. Higgins would be forthcoming with the chat.

"What do *you* want?" he mumbled between mouthfuls of hay. Not a good start.

"Hi, Mr. Higgins!" I said brightly. "Got anything you'd like to say? Anything you want me to tell Leanne? You know, something to communicate?"

"I know who you are. You're that freaky pony whis-pering girl the other ponies have been talking about," Mr. Higgins said in a bored, rather snooty voice. "Come to act as a go-between, have you?"

"Yes, that's right," I said.

"What's he saying?" asked Leanne, leaning closer.

"Nothing yet," I told her.

"Good," said Mr. Higgins, clearing his throat, "because you can tell her from me that I am sick to death of wearing these stupid rugs. Day rugs, night rugs, turnout rugs in several different weights and colors. Rugs for the dressage shows, a rug for traveling, a rug for the times between rugs. New rugs every year in all the latest colors and weights. I've got more rugs than they've got in Persia and they itch and pull and get on my nerves. Look at this one!" he said, nodding toward his chest. "Pulling across the shoulders and driving me crazy. It's ninety degrees outside, she's walking about in a crop top, and she insists on trussing me up in a rug. What's that about? Tell her to ditch the rugs!"

"What's he telling you?" asked Leanne.

"Well…"

"Come on, tell me," she insisted.

"He's a little upset at having to wear so many rugs," I said.

"What do you mean? He only wears one at a time."

"Mr. Higgins feels that his rug wardrobe is, erm, too extensive. He says the one he's wearing now itches and pulls across his chest, and he's fed up with you rugging him up morning, noon, and night—have I got that right?" I asked Mr. Higgins. He nodded.

"Spot on, Pony Whisperer!" he agreed, returning to his feed bag. I waited for Leanne to thank me. I'd done what she'd asked; she was bound to be grateful for the feedback. How wrong could I be? Leanne gave me a cold stare.

"You're asking me to believe *that's* what Mr. Higgins said?" she said, gritting her teeth.

"Huh?" I was confused.

"Do you honestly expect me to believe that's all my pony said to you? Are you just being mean?"

I was surprised. I'd done exactly what she'd asked and told her exactly what Mr. Higgins had asked me to. Why was she so upset? Leanne hadn't finished.

"I thought you would be a bigger person than that, Pia, but I see Catriona is right. You just make things up. I don't know why I bothered to ask you to talk to Mr. Higgins, and I don't know why you're being so nasty. Forget I ever asked you," she snapped, going into Mr. Higgins's stable and closing the door behind her.

I had been dismissed. What happened? She'd asked me; I'd delivered. I obviously hadn't said what Leanne had wanted to hear. But I couldn't just make things up—but maybe I should have.

Troubled, I was on my way to the barn once more to get Drummer's tack when Bethany's mom bore down on me, thrusting Pippin's lead rope into my hand. He was tacked up with Bethany on board.

"Can you hang on to him for just five seconds?" she asked me, holding up her spread hand to emphasize the five. "I've forgotten Bethany's gloves—they're in the car."

"OK," I agreed, stroking Pippin's white face. As her

mom ran off to the car, Bethany smiled shyly at me, her soft fair hair escaping from under her riding hat.

"Pippin's my pony, all mine," she said.

"That's right," I agreed. I never know what to say to small children, not having any brothers or sisters of my own.

"That's all very well now," said Pippin, gruffly. He looked quite angelic, but he was about thirty and creaked when he walked. "I've had at least fifteen owners, and they all thought they were the *only ones*," he continued. "I expect I'll be moving onto another child before very long. Another one bouncing up and down on my back and hauling on the reins. Who'd be a first pony? I'd buck if I had the energy."

"My pony, my pony, only mine," chanted Bethany. This was the longest five seconds in history. I wondered where her mom had gone.

"You know, Pippin's had a lot of other owners before you," I said, making conversation. "He says he's taught at least fifteen other lucky little girls to ride." I was sure she'd be thrilled to hear what her pony had to say. "And he says he hopes to teach lots more," I added, smiling.

Bethany stuck out her bottom lip. "No, only mine!" she repeated.

"Well, yes, he's yours *now*," I said, patting Pippin's neck. "But he's belonged to other little girls before you, and when you get too big for him, he'll have a new owner."

Bethany's face crumpled and she wailed, "Mine, he's no one else's, only mine." Tears started to flow. "He doesn't talk to you, he's mine!" she sobbed.

"Oh, for goodness' sake, shut her up!" implored Pippin, his ears shooting backward and forward, his eyes blinking in distress.

Bethany's mom came running back. "What's going on?" she demanded.

"Er...well...I..." I stammered. I didn't understand what had just happened. One minute Bethany had been fine; the next she was a screaming demon child.

"She says Pippin's going to teach other children to ride!" howled Bethany, pointing an accusing finger at me. "I don't want him to. He's mine!"

Bethany's mom looked at me accusingly. "What did you say?" she said.

"I just said that Pippin had taught lots of other children to ride and that he was looking forward to teaching more," I told her. "It's what he told me," I added.

"Oh, yes? Well, who asked you to stick your nose in?" Bethany's mom said, snatching the lead rope out of my hand and marching Pippin off. "Mind your own business next time!" she added over her shoulder, before turning back to Bethany.

"It's OK, darling, the nasty girl didn't mean it, she doesn't know anything about Pippin. He's just yours."

"Yeah, thanks for that, big mouth," added Pippin. "She'll be screaming for ages."

It clearly wasn't a good day for pony whispering.

Katy and I went for our ride. Bluey bent Drum's ear all the way around and Katy bent mine, asking me what Bluey was saying. Still smarting from my most recent pony whispering experiences, I avoided telling her. It was only the usual stuff—cross-country jumps Bluey had tackled and how cool it was. When we got back, word of my less-than-successful morning had spread.

"Why were you so mean to Leanne?" asked Dee.

"What do you mean?" Katy wanted to know.

"Pia told Leanne that Mr. Higgins hates his rugs," explained Dee.

"Did you? Why?" asked Katy.

"Because that's what he told me!" I said.

"Leanne said you were really smug and horrible about it," Dee said.

"I wasn't!" I protested.

"Why were you?" Katy said, aghast.

Bean joined in. "Bethany's been crying for ages," she said. "She says you told her terrible things about Pippin being sold. Why would you do that?"

"Oh, Pia, that's really mean," said Katy. "She's only a little kid."

"It wasn't like that at all," I protested. It didn't seem to matter what I said; I was already condemned. And then I noticed Catriona in Bambi's stable.

"Who told you, anyway?" I said.

"Well, Catriona said Leanne's very upset about what you said about Mr. Higgins," began Bean.

"Yes, and she said that Bethany's mom was going to tell Mrs. Collins you're a bad influence," added Dee.

"I didn't think you would be mean like that," mumbled Bean, going into Tiffany's stable, shaking her head.

Feeling wretched, I turned Drummer out in the field, giving him a big kiss and hugging him before letting him go.

"You have to be more careful about what you choose to tell people," advised Drum. "Take a leaf out of my book and keep quiet!"

"Do you mean that what I'm asking about Moth will be bad and not what I want to hear?" I asked him.

"You never give up, do you?" snorted Drummer, trotting off.

When I went to fetch my bike, I saw that James had arrived and was talking with Catriona. As he grinned and waved when he saw me and I waved back, I felt overwhelmed by guilt. I couldn't help liking James, but what if my worst fears about him were true? As I pedaled home, I knew I had a duty to find out because if I didn't, who would? I'd be failing Moth if I turned my back on my suspicions. I couldn't think why no one else at the yard hadn't noticed Moth's behavior. Thoughts raced around my head like a million bees buzzing around a hive. I felt quite worn out by it all.

When I got home, things weren't much better.

"I've got another date tonight, Pia," Mom said as I walked through the door. "You'll be OK for a couple of hours, won't you?"

"Yes, of course. Is it Gary again?" I tried to sound interested although my heart was sinking.

"Who? Oh, no, not Gary. This one's called Graham. He's retired."

"Jeez," I cried, "how old is he?"

"Some people take early retirement, you know!" Mom said, all indignant on Graham's behalf. "Besides, it'll be nice to feel young again, by comparison, I mean," she added, pulling a face at me.

"Oh, OK," I said, too wrapped up in my own woes to be interested.

"Are you all right?" Mom asked. She can usually tell when I'm down.

"Yes, fine," I lied, brightly. I managed to help Mom with her hair and wished her a great date as she went off, all swishy skirt and heels and looking nervous and excited at the same time. At least she wasn't the depressed and sad mother I'd had for so long. I just hoped this Graham wasn't a hit. I mean, retired! I didn't even want to think about a senior cluttering up the place, all pipe and slippers and coughing and wheezing, talking about the old days. Then I realized what a horrible daughter I was—it was all about me, wasn't it? Drum was right; I was always complaining about something. Shoving a pizza in the oven, I decided I'd buck up a bit and stop whining. I was starting to get on my own nerves.

Feeling a bit mean, I waited up for Mom and showed an interest—and she was full of her date—how Graham had been a real gentleman, how he'd talked about his own life (been in the army, run his own business, had three grown-up sons with children of their own, been divorced a number of years) but had shown a real interest in her and her life— and he was looking forward to meeting me (oh, no!). It was Graham this and Graham that until I was so fed up with hearing about awful Graham, I wish I'd been my usual selfish self and gone to bed earlier.

Just before I fell asleep, I decided I had to take control over my own life. No more complaining. I had to put a positive spin on things and get a grip. My mom was dating— great! I could talk to ponies—double great! So there were a few hang-ups that went with it, so what? The hang-ups would blow over; Drummer was right. Tomorrow would be better.

I really believed it, too…

CHAPTER 11

As I arrived at the yard the next day, I reminded myself that I was going to be positive. Yup, everything was just splendid. Fabulous. Great. Positive spin was what was needed. Drummer noticed the difference, too.

"You're chipper today," he yawned, as I slipped his halter around his ears and led him to the field gate.

"I'm making the best of things, being positive," I confided.

"Oh, I see. Good plan," Drummer replied, rubbing his face on a front leg.

Dee was in the barn when I went to get Drummer's grooming kit, and as part of my new positive strategy, I smiled broadly at her. She half smiled back, which I found encouraging. I mean, she could have turned her back on me or told me to get lost. With a deep breath, I decided that my positive policy was going to work.

As I brushed dust and grass off Drummer's shiny brown coat, other people started to arrive. A streak of purple, which I presumed to be Katy, ran out to the field to find Bluey, and Bean and Catriona arrived together in Bean's mom's car. Bean waved at me, but Catriona ignored me and disappeared into the tack room. I didn't hold any hopes of my positive policy working on her.

Suddenly, I heard strange voices. As Drummer had his head out over his half door and I was at the other end of him, spraying conditioner on his tail, he could see more than I could.

"Uh-oh," he said, softly, "something's amiss."

Pushing in, I looked over the half door with him. A stranger, a girl, was looking in the tack room.

"What do you want?" I heard Catriona say rudely.

"Nuthin'," said the girl. She was quite hefty with cropped blond hair with red streaks. I mean proper red, like Christmas red. Another girl, trailing along from the direction of the ponies' field, joined her. She wore striped jeans and a black sweater and her hair was clipped up behind her head. They both looked as hard as nails, the sort of girls you dreaded getting caught with at a bus stop. They looked like they'd steal your bus money and then decide they could do with a new cell phone. Yours.

"We've come to see the Pony Whisperer," said Red Streaks.

"Yeah, we know she hangs out here, so don't tell us no lies," added Striped Jeans.

I felt my stomach lurch. What did they want with me? I saw Catriona glance in my direction. She wasn't going to save me.

"The Pony Whispering Liar Girl is over there," she said, nodding. "But you do know you're on private property, don't you? You're not allowed on the place unless you keep a horse here."

"Who's gonna know?" said Red Streaks belligerently, striding over to Drummer's stable, her friend in tow.

"What have you done now?" hissed Drummer.

"No idea," I hissed back.

"You the Pony Whisperer?" asked Red Streaks.

"Yeah, she is. I recognize her from TV," said Striped Jeans.

"You can hear what horses say, then?" Red Streaks continued.

"Er…" I didn't know what to say. So I nodded. "Yes, I can," I said, gulping.

"Cool!" exclaimed Striped Jeans, grinning.

"Give us your autograph," said Red Streaks, whipping out an autograph book.

"What?" I was flabbergasted. My *autograph?* They had to be kidding.

"Yeah, and me," said Striped Jeans, handing me a pen.

"Give me a break. Your autograph? Whatever next?" said Drummer, backing away from the door in disgust.

I looked across at Catriona. She was watching, probably hoping I was going to get beaten up by the hard nuts. When she realized they had come for my autograph, she narrowed her eyes and pressed her lips together. Not a happy camper. As I signed my name next to a couple of lesser known pop stars, a soap actor, and a stand-up comedian, I saw Catriona run over and knock on Mrs. Collins's front door.

"Are there a lot of horses here?" asked Striped Jeans, looking around.

"I suppose you have to be rich to have a horse?" said Red Streaks.

"Can I help you, girls?" Mrs. Collins arrived with Squish in tow. She didn't look very pleased. Squish pushed his head under Striped Jeans's hand to be stroked. Guard dog he wasn't.

"Come to see the famous Pony Whisperer," said Red Streaks.

"Well, this is private property, so you'll have to leave," said Mrs. C.

"That's not very friendly," Red Streaks cried.

"Can't you tell her we're your friends?" asked Striped Jeans, turning to me.

"Er…well…" I stammered. This was getting awkward.

"No, you're not," said Mrs. Collins, firmly. "And how did you know Pia kept her pony here, anyway?"

"Oh, well, things get out," replied Red Streaks.

"Yeah, we've got friends who know about this place," Striped Jeans bragged.

"Come on, Gemma," said Red Streaks, "we can tell where we're not wanted. We got what we come for."

"But what about—" began Striped Jeans, looking back toward the field.

"Leave it, Gemma!" warned Red Streaks.

The girls sauntered off down the drive. It was a mystery. After all, you can't see the yard from the road, and I didn't understand how they could possibly have known I kept Drummer there.

"This isn't good enough, Pia," warned Mrs. Collins. "We can't have strangers wandering about. There are some valuable animals here, not to mention the tack. Don't invite anyone else but your immediate family in the future."

"But I didn't invite them!" I said. "I've never seen them before in my life!"

"Well, any more of this kind of unwanted attention, and I may have to ask you to leave," was Mrs. C's parting shot as she padded back to her house in her slippers, Squish behind her. Cat smirked at me.

"If my tack gets nicked, Ma-*ria*," she said, menacingly, "I'll expect you to buy me some more."

I was *so* getting fed up with Cat calling me by the wrong name. I had wondered whether I could think up a nickname for her—Whiskers or Kitty Cat or something—but they sounded so stupid and childish, and I had decided I'd try to rise above it and have a stab at being mature. It wasn't easy...

Bean and Katy returned to the yard, towing Tiffany and Bluey behind them. Thank goodness, I thought. My relief didn't last long.

"There are some rough-looking boys hanging around in the field," announced Bean.

"I'm going to get Mrs. Collins to get rid of them," said Katy. "They're not taking any notice of us."

"I expect they're come to see Ma-*ria*, here," said Catriona.

"Who?" asked Bean, pausing in midstride, her hand poised above Mrs. Collins's doorbell.

"Our little celebrity is being hounded by her fans. We've just had to evict two pathetic girls who wanted *the Pony*

Whisperer's autograph," she explained. "The boys must be with them."

Katy's eyes were like saucers. "Oh, how exciting!" she said, patting Bluey's neck.

"Not really," contradicted Cat. "Mrs. Collins is furious. She's a security risk. I mean, think of the tack, not to mention the ponies. How would you feel if you came up one day to find the place cleaned out and our ponies all stolen?"

Bean and Katy looked at me. I gulped again.

"Oh, no!" said Bean. "I'll get Mrs. C."

So Mrs. Collins came out again and had to shoo off the rough-looking boys who had climbed over the fence into the field and were hanging around the gate. One of them was smoking and the other shouted something very rude back. They didn't look exactly like the horse thieves Catriona had them down as, but you never can tell.

"We only wanted to see the girl on TV!" one of them shouted as they walked off down the drive after the girls, throwing their chewing gum onto the gravel and breaking branches off the trees.

"You're a big pain, aren't you?" said Catriona. She wasn't going to let it end there—particularly as James had turned up.

"What's with the punks?" he said. He'd passed them on the way in.

"Ask your pony-lying-whispering friend," spat Catriona.

"They've come to see me, apparently," I said, guiltily.

"Got a fan club, have you?" James asked. He'd got it immediately.

"See? Now she's a security risk," said Catriona, twisting the knife.

"Oh, well, you can't blame people for being nosy," said James. "I don't suppose she represents much of a risk, really."

"Well, there is the tack," Bean pointed out. "I mean, it's very valuable."

"And it's under lock and key!" said James, gallantly fighting my battle for me, which made me feel even worse for harboring nasty suspicions about him. But then I remembered that he could just be stocking up points and trying to throw me off the scent, just in case Moth told me everything. God, he was a sly one.

"Still, you can't see anything from the road; no one would know horses and ponies were kept here," Katy said.

"No, of course not," agreed James, "unless you happened to see us all trotting in and out of the drive on our ponies. Not rocket science, is it?"

Everyone wandered off and got on with grooming, catching ponies, and mucking out.

"Celebrity," said Drum, swishing his tail and grunting. "I dunno, it's not all it's cracked up to be, is it?"

"Oh, what do you know?" I said irritably.

"Well, you've got to take the rough with the smooth," Drum said, smugly. "Though I must say, James stuck up for you. What's that about?"

I felt a slight flutter—followed by a pang of guilt. But surely James was too nice to abuse Moth? But then when murderers were caught, there were always neighbors on the TV saying what a nice guy he'd been, so polite and nice to the kids and how much they'd liked him. He was always the last person the neighbors would have suspected. I had to remember that. And I just couldn't like anyone who would hurt a horse or pony. Poor Moth.

"I wish everyone would just leave me alone," I muttered, annoyed and confused by my own thoughts.

"Tut, tut!" exclaimed Drummer, in a maddening way. "I thought you were going to be positive today? That didn't last long."

"I am being positive!" I exclaimed. "I *positively* wish everyone would leave me alone!"

Leanne and Cat went off riding together, and I could hear them talking about me as they rode down the drive. What a pain I was. What a security risk. What was Mrs. Collins thinking of, letting me stay? I hoped they didn't persuade Mrs. C otherwise. I had hated coming to this new yard, but now we'd got to know some of the people and ponies here, I really wanted to stay. I imagined having to find another yard, going through the same thing again—and at every yard there would be a Catriona, but not necessarily a James—one who loved his pony, anyway.

I jumped about three feet in the air when James's head bobbed around Drummer's top door.

"You're quiet!" he said, shoving his hair back from his face.

"Well, I was going to be positive today, but recent events have put that plan under severe pressure," I explained. My voice sounded funny—I wanted to distance myself from James, but it was so hard.

"Hey, don't worry. It'll blow over."

"Mrs. Collins said she'd throw me out if it happened again," I said, glumly. "And Drum's settled in nicely here. I'd hate to take him away when he's made friends."

"It won't come to that. I've lost count of the number of times Mrs. C's threatened to throw me out. It's her favorite thing to say! Take no notice."

"Really?" I asked. "You're not just trying to make me feel better?" I could feel myself warming to him again. I was useless!

"No, honest. And cheer up, no one would like to see you leave," James continued. "Katy likes you, and Bean. Dee-Dee says you're cool, too. Everyone likes you, honestly."

"Except Cat!" I pointed out.

"You can't expect a one-hundred-percent hit rate!" laughed James. "Don't worry, she'll come 'round eventually. I bet in a couple of weeks, you two will be best buddies."

It was obvious that James didn't understand how girls worked. If Cat and I were boys, James's prediction would probably come true. As it was…

"Don't worry too much about Catriona," continued James. "She'd do *anything* to have your gift. I expect we all would."

Anything? I felt a chill run up my spine. I had to make sure Catriona never discovered the secret of Epona. Or

James. I had to hand it to him, he knew how to get around people. I couldn't let that happen; I couldn't get my fears for Moth out of my mind. If only I had some proof.

When I got home, I thought I'd have a nice, quiet night. I'd have dinner, do some homework, and then go to bed and read a book. I had a couple of paperbacks I'd got for Christmas still waiting to be read that I had only just found after the move and that would put thoughts of Epona, Catriona, and James right out of my mind. Mmm, yes, a peaceful night.

Wrong. The moment I set foot through the front door I heard voices. One was my mom's; the other definitely wasn't. My heart sank.

"Hello!" I yelled. I knew what was coming and I didn't want to overhear anything I'd rather keep secret. Mom and a tall, dark-haired man with a moustache emerged from the kitchen. He wore brown corduroy trousers over suede shoes and a checked, long-sleeved shirt and brown tie. He looked miles older than Mom.

"Pia!" exclaimed Mom, like I was a surprise even though I do live there! "This is Graham, who I told you about. We're going out again tonight."

Graham nodded toward me. "Hello there," he said. "I've been looking forward to meeting you, young Pia. Your lovely mother has been telling me all about you."

Oh, dear, I thought, that's a shame. He stood very stiffly, like he was standing to attention, and he spoke quite loudly, like he was addressing a crowd. Before I could reply, Mom, grinning from ear to ear, launched herself at me. "Oh, Pia, you'll never guess what!" she said, all excited.

I braced myself. What else could there be?

"OK, let me have it!" I said.

"The TV company called again. There was such a lot of interest in you when you appeared on the Cecily Armstrong show, they want to do a one-off special. Just you!"

My heart sank. I had wanted to be a celebrity; now I wondered how another TV appearance would rate at the yard. I *so* didn't want to be kicked out.

"So of course, I said you'd do it—we so enjoyed the last one," Mom explained to Graham.

"What?"

"Oh, come on, you know you'll love it. It's on Saturday, so you won't have to get permission from school."

"Saturday? That's only two days away!"

"Yes, good, isn't it? They want you to do your pony whispering thing live on air. That's what they're going to call it, *Pony Whispering Live!* They've got a couple of horses with problems, and they want you to go and talk to them and sort them out. Isn't it exciting? My daughter, a TV star!" She said the last bit to Graham and he launched an insincere smile in my direction.

"Your mother is very proud of you, Pia," he said. "It seems you are a rather gifted and creative child." It was clear he thought I was making it up. Not that his opinion mattered.

Mom went on and on and on. And on. Then she went too far and invited Graham along on Saturday. Graham agreed, saying it was only right that a man ought to accompany two young ladies, which I thought was a real liberty. Who did he think he was? Like we couldn't go without him! But Mom, instead of telling him to get lost, went all Jane Austen at him, fluttering her eyelashes and saying it would be good to have a strong man along—I couldn't believe it. We didn't need him! And then they went off on their date—Graham making a big thing of opening the door for Mom to go through and Mom thanking him and going all fluttery again.

Double pooh.

How could Mom like anyone so, so *boring* and so old-fashioned? And how *could* she have invited him to come with us on Saturday? Although it might at least stop her from flirting with everyone like last time. And why did she turn into a simpering idiot-woman when he was being such a pompous old nitwit? She was never like that with Dad. But the biggest question of all was how was I going to get through this *Pony Whispering Live!?*

Quadruple pooh!

Squared!

CHAPTER 12

P*ONY WHISPERING LIVE!* DAY dawned bright and warm. I'd been awake for half of the night, worrying about it. What if I couldn't help the horses they had lined up? What if I said it all wrong, like I had about Mr. Higgins and Pippin, and everybody hated me? What if I got a pony like Moth—silent and anything but forthcoming? What if? What if? What if?

Mom was overexcited.

"I've told your father about it," she said, shoveling Special K down her throat. "He was a little upset at not knowing about your first TV performance so I had to tell him so he can watch it this afternoon. He wanted to know all about it. Funny how he wants to know all about your TV appearances and nothing much about anything else!"

"I have to check on Drummer before we go," I told her. "Can you pick me up from the yard?"

"OK, but be ready—Graham and I will be there at eleven. We have to be at this other yard, Highfield Liveries, by twelve."

What to wear? I'd been agonizing over my wardrobe ever since Mom had broken the news, but I still changed my mind twice this morning. Should I wear riding clothes? Too geeky. Jeans? Too casual. Goldilocks was more decisive than me. I went for a nice pair of black jeans with a white T-shirt, topped with a jacket. Did I look smart yet casual? Looking in the mirror I decided that I did. Well, sort of.

I got Epona out and gave her a stiff talking-to.

"I know you didn't get me into this," I said, "and that it's all my own fault, but I hope you can give me a couple of easy ponies to deal with today. I need some help, here!"

Epona, unsurprisingly, said nothing. I rubbed where her nose had been, and then I stroked the horse she was riding for luck before putting her in my jacket pocket and peddling to the yard.

James was grooming Moth outside his stable. Moth stood there with her head high, as usual, looking anything but relaxed as James brushed her mane. I didn't want to think about Moth's problems today—they were too exhausting. Besides, I had enough of my own.

"Dressed up a bit, aren't you?" observed James.

"Mmmm, I've got a TV thing to do," I explained in my distant voice I reserved for James. I couldn't be friendly; it wasn't right.

"That *Pony Whispering Live!* gig? Bean told me about it," said James, moving on to Moth's tail.

I'd told Katy and Bean about the show. They'd obviously been sharing.

"It's at Highfield Liveries, isn't it? Fancy place! Hope it goes well," said James, wiping his arm across his brow. "Phew, it's hot today. I think we'll go down to the river, eh, Moth? Shame you and Drummer can't come with us," he added.

Oh, if only! Then I felt awful. Even with my suspicions about James, I still wanted to go riding with him. If only he wasn't so cute. My mind was completely churned up with all my conflicting thoughts.

I found Drummer grazing alone by the water trough.

"Hello, you," I said.

"Oh, hi," he said, lifting his head and accepting the carrot I'd brought him.

"Can't stop, got this TV thing to do today," I explained. It sounded weird.

"Oh, shame," said Drummer, sarcastically. "Does that mean I get the day off?"

"Looks like it, have a good one. Wish me luck."

"OK, good luck." Drummer went back to grazing and I returned to the yard. It was so hot already! I looked at my watch. Ten minutes before Mom was due. I just had time to clean out Drummer's water buckets—that would cool me down. I carefully hung my jacket on Drummer's door to keep it clean, and then I sloshed some water about, turning Drum's buckets upside down afterward to dry out and air. That was another job done—and only just in time for I heard Mom toot her car horn as she bumped her way along the drive. Graham was sitting next to her in his corduroy trousers and a different shirt. Still checked, though, I noticed. He was obviously a man who knew what he liked. I hoped he didn't take too much of a liking to my mom.

"Come on!" she yelled out of the window, and I jumped into the backseat, annoyed to be relegated there by the pompous moustache.

"OK?" Mom asked, looking at me in the rearview mirror. I nodded.

"You look terrific!" I said. And she did. She was wearing dark green pants and a white blouse and her hair was tied back with a dark green scarf. I just hoped no one would ply her with wine.

Highfield Liveries was one of those fabulous stable yards built in a square, with an archway complete with a clock, a concrete apron outside the stable doors, and manicured grass in the middle. It was obvious no one ever, ever strayed onto it—there wasn't a hoofprint in sight. The whole place was immaculate; it had brass nameplates on every door, a rug room, a washing room—even an equine solarium. I gulped—what a place! A notice advised visitors about the fire drill, and more notices were in prominent places. I mean proper, painted notices, not scraps of paper with wobbly handwriting pinned to the wall like at our yard. They even had grooms—in navy sweatshirts and jodhpurs. I mean, how cool is that? And there, by the fire drill notice, looking completely out of place and self-conscious were two people I hadn't expected to see: my dad and Skinny Lynny.

"Oh, no!" I heard Mom mutter. "Me and my big mouth."

"Hi, Pumpkin!" cried Dad, waving.

"Yoo-hoo, Pia!" said Skinny Lynny, smiling. She was

149

wearing a very, very short skirt with a tiny spotted top and sandals. Her hair, as always, was poker straight, and huge designer sunglasses sat on the top of her head. I didn't know what the outfit had cost, but I bet it was at least equal to Drum's keep for a month *and* a visit from the farrier. But then, as Mom was always pointing out, his salary is obviously one of the things that Skinny Lynny finds so attractive about my dad.

There was the usual strained exchange of greetings among Mom, Dad, and Skinny Lynny, with Mom introducing Graham, who shook everyone's hand, his eyes almost popping out of his head when he saw Skinny Lynny, and then they turned to me.

"I am so proud of you, Pia," said Dad. He looked quite emotional. "You have this amazing gift. It's just wonderful; it really is."

My heart sank. My father was proud of me—for lying. If he only knew. Guilt gripped me again. I couldn't keep doing this.

"Which are the *important* TV people?" asked Skinny Lynny, glancing around. She looked even skinnier than usual. If she lost any more weight, I thought, she'd disappear altogether. I wondered whether that was possible because that would be a great result. I suddenly realized she had come only to be noticed. It wasn't about me at all, but about Skinny Lynny being discovered. Discovered for what, I had no idea. Skinniest person on the planet? Stepmother from hell? I looked at Mom. She really did look pretty good—not as young or as slim as Skinny Lynny, but well dressed and well groomed. I was really proud of her. No longer plump and frumpy, she had certainly made herself over. I wondered whether Dad had noticed, too. Whether he would—

"You must be Pia!" a good-looking man with twinkling blue eyes interrupted my optimistic dreams. "I'm Howard Slater. I'm hosting *Pony Whispering Live!*"

"Oh, I recognize you," interrupted Skinny Lynny in her breathy, little girl voice. She stroked her neck and smiled at Howard. "Don't you do *Get the Look*, the program all about affordable designer looks for your home?"

"Well, yes, I do!" said Howard, tapping the tiny microphone he had in one ear and listening intently. "OK," he said to whoever was speaking to him. "Gotta go!" he explained, taking my elbow and steering me away, leaving the uncomfortable foursome to their own devices.

"So, *Pony Whispering Live!*" Howard said. "We've got a horse and a pony with hang-ups. Their owners have tried all sorts of things—but the hang-ups are still there, apparently. So we'd just like you to do your thing with them—find out what their problems are."

For the umpteenth time I considered whether I was doing the right thing, keeping the truth of my pony whispering ability a secret. But if I could do anything to help, then surely it was my duty to try—even allowing for my failings with Moth. My conscience eased a bit. And anyway, I could always make some stuff up—who

151

would know the difference? Howard seemed able to read my evil thoughts.

"We've got a research team to verify your findings," he said, waving his hand toward two women—one with a cell phone and another with a laptop. They grinned and nodded at me.

"What?" I said. A research team? What did that mean?

"If you discover anything about a horse—previous owners, what they used to do, these girls can check it out."

Oh, pooh.

Suddenly everything started happening.

"Right, everyone!" Almost time. "Howard, are you ready?" shouted someone from by the TV.

Howard nodded and led me to the grass in middle of the yard. The sun beat down on us and someone pinned a microphone to my T-shirt and then did the same to Howard. Other people bustled around looking busy.

"Five minutes," said Howard, nodding at me.

Silence fell. I could see my family (and Skinny Lynny and Graham, I thought, unable to include them as family) watching quietly, could see the uniformed grooms in a huddle, could see another group of people, probably the owners of the other horses and ponies stabled there, watching, too. Equine heads, curious about the happenings in their yard, looked out over the half doors.

Something was wrong. It was *so* quiet. Something wasn't right. What *was* it? I couldn't think why I felt so sort of… well, sort of…incomplete. Something was missing. What?

It was too quiet.

I couldn't hear anything.

No voices.

No *equine* voices.

Sweat broke out on my forehead and my legs went wobbly. I realized in a horrible, heart-stopping instant that there was no way I could do what I was there to do. *Pony Whispering Live!* was going to be a complete and utter TV flop, everyone would know I'd been lying, but most of all, Catriona was going to be so, so thrilled at my failure.

Because Epona was in my jacket pocket.

And my jacket was swinging from Drummer's stable door.

CHAPTER 13

WHAT WAS I GOING to do? No Epona equaled no *Pony Whispering Live!* My mind raced. How could I get to the yard and retrieve my jacket? There was no time. I'd have to wing it, to make it all up. But that wouldn't work—not with the research team waiting to catch me.

And then the worst thought of all: What if Catriona picked up my jacket? Oh, please no. Anything but that. Epona in Catriona's hands? A wave of despair swept over me. I couldn't lose Epona to Catriona; it was unthinkable.

"OK?" asked Howard.

I couldn't speak. My throat felt as though someone had tipped the Sahara Desert into it. Think, Pia! I told myself. But I couldn't think because all I could hear was a thudding in my head. Except when I looked up, it wasn't in my head; it was the real sound of galloping hooves. Everyone turned to see a pony canter through the gates and over the carpet of grass toward us, its mane and tail flying. Howard nipped behind me nervously—clearly he wasn't used to horses.

The ground shook as the pony thundered toward us and then slid to a stop, its rider launching himself out of the saddle toward me. What were they doing here? What...?

How…? My head was spinning and I couldn't move; it was all too surreal.

Throwing one arm around me, the rider squeezed me tight and planted a big kiss on my cheek. It was a good thing my throat was full of the Sahara because the rider was James.

"Hi, sweetheart!" he exclaimed, oblivious to my wide-eyed, rabbit-caught-in-the-headlights expression. "I just *had* to wish you good luck!"

I felt him press something into my hand. It was rough and made of stone and as soon as I felt it in my sweating palm, I heard the murmur of all the horses and ponies around me.

Epona!

"Oh, thank you!" I whispered, my suspicions about James suspended by utter relief. "Thank you, thank you."

James turned to Howard and winked. "I'm her boy-friend," he explained in a man-to-man voice as he swung himself back into Moth's saddle, cantering over the grass and out of the yard again like it was the most natural thing in the world. Everyone saw a boy on a chestnut cob, but I saw a knight in shining armor on a perfect charger, riding away after having saved his (rather forgetful) damsel from distress. I could see the TV people all looking furious, could see hoofprints all across the previously immaculate grass in the yard, but I didn't care. It didn't matter what happened now that I had Epona back.

"Sorry about that," I said, shoving Epona into the pocket of my jeans.

"Do you expect anyone else to come and offer their support?" the man who'd been introduced as the producer yelled sarcastically.

"No, no one. Sorry," I said again.

The director counted down and Howard smiled into the camera and introduced me, explaining about *Pony Whispering Live!* We were on! Then a girl about my age with short blond hair and dressed in riding clothes led a pony with a spotless white coat and oiled hooves toward us.

"This is Seagull," explained Howard, "and her owner Holly. Tell us about Seagull's problem, Holly."

"Seagull is such a darling," started Holly, nervously, "but she just freaks out now and again. Nobody can understand it. She shakes and she shivers and if I'm riding her, she tries to bolt with me. If she's in the stable, she gets all agitated and races around. I'm scared she's going to hurt herself, and my mom's worried she'll hurt *me*. The vet's baffled and can't find anything wrong. The strange thing is, it usually happens on Saturdays—like today, but she sometimes does it on other days, too. We don't know what's wrong!"

I looked at Seagull. The gray looked quite calm and serene, almost bored. Why did she suddenly flip now and again? And why did it happen on Saturdays? Putting my hand on Seagull's neck, I spoke to her.

"Hi, Seagull, won't you tell me why you behave so strangely now and again?" I said. I felt a bit stupid with everyone standing there, watching.

Seagull sighed. "Like you'd know anything about it!" she remarked.

"Actually, I would," I said. "I can hear every word you're saying."

Seagull turned her head and looked me in the eye. Howard caught his breath and told the camera that it looked as though Seagull was going to talk to the Pony Whisperer.

And then, right on cue, Seagull freaked out. Up went her head, her ears flicked back and forth, and she dragged poor Holly along the yard, ignoring her soothing words. Two grooms rushed in to help, virtually pinning the pony down as Howard, the cameraman, and me all hurried along to catch up.

"Make them stop, make them stop!" cried Seagull, trembling and terrified. I felt really sorry for her—whatever was making her so scared? Nothing had changed; it was as though she was possessed by demons.

"Seagull," I said, "tell me what you're so scared of. What's happened?"

"I can hear them. We're going to have to charge!"

"No one is going to hurt you," I told her. "If you can just tell me, we want to help you. Please, Seagull!" I really felt for her. The pony was clearly terrified—but of what?

"Don't make me charge!" she repeated.

"What is she saying?" asked Holly, her eyes wide. "Tell us!"

"She says she doesn't want to *charge*," I repeated. It didn't make sense. Everyone just looked at one another, baffled.

"Why don't you want to charge, Seagull?" I asked, gently.

"We're galloping together, I can hear the shouts and the thunder of galloping hooves around me, but then the guns start to fire, and my friends start to fall. We charge on and on—and it gets worse, it gets worse."

Emma Ellison, the horse healer, popped into my mind. Something she had said when we'd been on the television together, about a horse she had helped, a horse that had been a bullfighting horse in a former life. It was worth a guess.

"Are you a *warhorse?*" I asked, incredulously. How could a pony be caught up in war? Then I had an idea.

"What's your name?" I asked. Holly mumbled something about her being called Seagull and looking at Howard as though I was mad, but the long shot could work.

"I am Wexford," said Seagull. "We crossed the sea, we marched for months, getting weaker and weaker—there was little food. And then we charged, galloping through the valley. But the guns were there, and my friends fell all around me."

"Wexford," I asked gently, "why are you so scared of charging now? Why right now?"

"I can hear the guns. We're going to have to charge."

I turned to Holly and Howard. "It seems that Seagull has lived before. She says she was Wexford, a cavalry charger."

Howard got very excited. "Where?" he hissed. "When? Which battle?"

I turned back to Seagull. "Where did you charge, Wexford? Do you know which battle it was?"

"I don't know," Seagull replied. "Make the guns stop, make them *stop!*"

"She says she can hear guns," I said. I wasn't making much sense. What guns? I couldn't hear anything.

"Oh!" said one of the grooms, her mouth dropping open. "The clay pigeon shoot! It always takes place on Saturdays, and sometimes during the week or on holidays. It's miles away, but when the wind is in the right direction, you can just hear the shotguns."

There followed a deathly hush as everyone listened, straining to hear.

"I can't hear anything," said Howard.

"But ponies' hearing is much more sensitive than ours," explained Holly.

Howard swung around to the research team. "Can you find out whether the clay pigeon shoot is on today? Right now?" he asked.

"It takes place at Home Farm," said the groom.

Howard looked into the camera. "Can Seagull really have lived the life of a cavalry charger? Find out whether the Pony Whisperer has discovered the secret of this poor pony's despair after the break."

"Three minutes!" shouted the director.

"That's amazing!" said Howard, wiping his brow.

"My poor, poor Seagull," Holly whispered. She turned to me. "If you're right, I'll find a place to keep her where she won't hear any guns. She must be terrified." She and the grooms manhandled poor Seagull back to her stable.

The gray mare tore around the inside, clearly agitated. It was really sad. I thought briefly of batty Emma Ellison, the healer I'd met during my last TV appearance. I had thought she was bonkers, talking about the horses she had healed. Maybe she wasn't so crazy, after all. Maybe she did a good job with ponies like Seagull.

One of the researchers handed Howard a piece of paper.

"Let's go, people," yelled the director. "Three, two, one…"

Howard spoke directly to the camera, glancing down at the paper he'd been given.

"Welcome back to part two of *Pony Whispering Live!* In part one we met Seagull, a pony who had unexplained fits. After communicating with Seagull, Pia Edwards, the Pony Whisperer, discovered the pony had lived before as a cavalry charger called Wexford and was terrified of the sound of guns. Now although *we* can't hear gunfire, our researcher has discovered that the weekly clay pigeon shoot several miles away started at exactly the same time Seagull became agitated this morning. Clearly, the Pony Whisperer knows her stuff. Who else could have discovered such an amazing story except someone in direct communication with Seagull herself? Astonishing!"

I was pretty astonished myself. Poor, poor Seagull. I didn't have time to dwell on her, however, as Howard had moved on. A stunningly beautiful woman led a big black horse across the yard to us. I wondered whether everyone on this yard had to pass a glamorous test before they could keep their horses there.

"Meet Penny and her show jumper, Ebony. Tell us what Ebony's problem is, Penny," said Howard.

"We're at our wits' end," started Penny. "Ebony just hates being out in the field. We did wonder whether he was agoraphobic, you know, scared of open spaces, and we've had a few healers out to see him, but they haven't been able to help. He's always turned out with a darling little Shetland, so he's not seeking company, but the moment we take our eyes off them both, Ebony jumps out of the field."

I gave Epona a tweak. How would we do with this one? I wondered.

"Hi, Ebony!" I started, brightly, stretching up to pat his gleaming black neck. He was a huge black horse with four white socks and a crooked white blaze that made his face look askew. Ebony stared straight ahead like I didn't exist.

"Ebony," I tried again, "I hear you keep jumping out of your field. Can you explain to me why you do this? Penny's very worried about you."

Ebony sighed. "Not another one who thinks she can reach my mind. Why don't you people go and get a hobby, keep fish, or take up knitting or something, instead of pretending to be mystics and bothering me?"

"I don't much like fish, and I'd rather do nothing at all than knit, thank you," I told him. That got his attention. It also made Howard and Penny look at me like I was nuts. Ebony turned his head and stared at me.

"Well, you're a welcome change!" he said, chuckling to himself. "Someone who *can* hear me. What a surprise! What do you want?"

"You're jumping out of your field, I understand," I said, very matter-of-factly. With Epona in my pocket and Seagull under my belt, my confidence was sky-high. "Can you tell me why? Are you agoraphobic, you know, scared of open spaces?"

"I know what agoraphobic means!" Ebony retorted. "And I'm not, thank you. The problem is that piebald demon, my so-called companion, Humbug. He hates me."

That floored me. I decided to share the information.

"He says he's not agoraphobic, but that the problem is his companion."

Penny shook her head. "His companion is a Shetland pony, comes up to Ebony's knees. How can he be a problem?"

"Ebony, what makes you think Humbug hates you?" I asked.

"He's a nasty piece of work," said Ebony, shivering. "He nips my knees and he kicks my hocks and he chases me around. He only does it when nobody's watching."

"But he's tiny!" I said.

"Look, I'm not proud of it, you know. OK, so he's small, but he's *evil*. He enjoys intimidating me. I'm a big horse, but I'm not one for violence—ask anyone, they'll tell you I'm a gentle giant. And he…well, he's very…*dominant!*"

"And that's why you jump out of the field?" I said. I wanted to get it right.

Ebony sighed like I was the slowest, dimmest person he had ever encountered. "Yes. Go on, rub it in. Like I said, I'm not proud of it. I'd rather run away than be violent toward another living creature. It's just not in my nature."

"Oh," I said. I turned to Howard and Penny. Both were leaning forward, waiting to hear what I had to say.

"Gentle giant Ebony here is being intimidated by the Shetland pony you turn him out with. It appears he's not such a good companion, after all."

"Little Humbug?" cried Penny in disbelief.

"Let's turn them out and see," suggested Howard. Penny led Ebony out to the field while one of the grooms fetched the accused—a tiny piebald Shetland with a mane like a mop and legs as long as rolling pins. Meanwhile, Howard kept the audience up to speed by explaining our strategy to the camera. Everyone trooped across to the field and stood by the fence, and Ebony sidled up to me.

"Why are you turning me out with him?" the black horse asked me in a hushed tone so that the Shetland couldn't hear. "I told you what was happening!"

"I know," I whispered over the fence, "but no one believes us."

"Oh, well, why ask then?" said Ebony. He had a point. "It's no good watching," he continued. "Little Humbug here is sweetness and light whenever anyone's about. He only turns into the Shetland from hell when we're alone so having the equivalent of a derby crowd all hanging over the fence won't prove anything. I mean, why don't you do a proper job—set up a couple of trade stands, invite the fairground over, sell hot dogs and souvenirs?"

Taking this in, I put across Ebony's point, leaving out the sarcasm, and everyone trooped off again, hovering behind the stables. The cameraman inched his handheld camera around the corner and Howard whispered into the microphone.

Nothing happened for a while and then, after looking around and seeing that everyone had gone, the piebald Shetland put his head down and charged, squealing and kicking up his heels at Ebony. He nipped his knees and tummy, he kicked out at his legs, he snaked his head up and down, threatening him with his teeth. Ebony bounced into a canter and cleared the fence easily.

"That's impressive!" I said.

"She's done it again, viewers," gasped Howard, clutching my elbow and swinging me around to face the camera. "The Pony Whisperer has solved the mystery. She's unbelievable!"

"Erm, would anyone like a cute little piebald Shetland?" mumbled Penny. "Free to a good home."

Don't hold your breath, I thought.

Howard worked the camera again. "Well, you saw it for yourselves, on *Pony Whispering Live!* this afternoon. The Pony Whisperer discovered the amazing secrets of both our featured horses..." He touched his earpiece, listening to some information coming through. "How extraordinary! Our research team has been in touch with the army records office, and it seems that they have discovered that a cavalry charger called Wexford was with the 17th Lancers, part of the famous Charge of the Light Brigade that was cut down by a Russian battery of twelve-pounder guns at Balaclava in October 1854, during the Crimean War. It seems poor Wexford fell there—as did 469 other horses that fateful day. Can it really be that little Seagull is a reincarnation of that courageous and loyal horse that battled so bravely with his equine friends and watched them fall around him?"

I shivered. Poor Seagull, taken back to the horror of a former life by the sound of a clay pigeon shoot. If Holly could move her to a place where the shoot was out of ear-shot, maybe Seagull would never again regress to being Wexford. How amazing that the researchers had discovered the truth.

Howard asked me to sum up my feelings and I mumbled something about being surprised about the way things had gone. Howard gushed about what he called my unique talent, to which I shrugged a bit and smiled and said I was very happy to help, and *Pony Whispering Live!* was suddenly all over. Phew!

The film crew were impressed and congratulated one another on a great show; I was thanked by Howard, the producer, Holly, and Penny; and a groom shook me by the hand and said I was just amazing!

That was the easy bit, I thought grimly, turning to my family who were standing by the yard gates with a crowd of people. Now I had to face Mom and Graham, Dad and

Skinny Lynny. Taking a deep breath, I walked over to them. But instead of the usual catty remarks (my mom) and deep sighs (my dad) and thin-lipped smiles (Skinny Lynny) that greeted me when they were forced together, they were all united, for once.

"That was fantastic!" said Dad.

"Pia, how can you possibly communicate with those poor horses?" asked Mom. Her eyes were red and it turned out she'd shed a tear for poor Seagull/Wexford.

"If you want to know more about the Charge of the Light Brigade," said Graham, bristling with importance, "I happen to be quite an authority on the Crimean War."

"Imagine being able to talk with those poor, poor little horses," breathed Skinny Lynny, not quite focusing her full attention on me, but glancing anxiously toward the film crew. She wasn't giving up.

"Now, Pia, it's all decided," Dad began, rubbing his hands together, "your mother has agreed that you'll come out with us right now to celebrate. We've hardly seen you since you've moved, so let's go and have a first-rate meal somewhere and you can tell us all about your pony whispering secrets."

"Yes," agreed Mom, kissing me on the cheek, "go and enjoy yourself. I'm really proud of you, Pia. Who would have thought you would be so, well, so unique!"

"Thanks, Mom," I said. I didn't want to go for a meal, first-rate or otherwise, with Skinny Lynny, but going back with Mom and Graham wasn't so appealing either—especially if

166

Graham was going to blather on about the Crimean War. I wished it could just be me and Dad, especially as Skinny's idea of a good meal was probably two lettuce leaves and a slice of cucumber. Fat chance.

I waved Mom and Graham off and then got into Dad's car. Skinny Lynny sat in the front, naturally, so again I was consigned to the back. Skinny twisted in the seat to look around at me.

"There's a darling little place near here—it specializes in shellfish. We can order a bottle of champagne, can't we, Paul?"

"Can't we just go to Pizza Hut?" I said.

"But this is a special occasion," said Skinny, dismayed.

"Pia never really liked shellfish," Dad chimed in, sticking up for me.

"I just *love* shellfish," said Skinny.

You mean you love being *selfish*, I thought.

"How about we compromise with a nice Italian restaurant?" Dad suggested, and we all agreed.

And it wasn't bad, after all. We did have champagne, and Skinny ordered squid—I tried some and it tasted like rubber bands. I had a massive pizza with hot chilies, which I scraped off because I only like where they've been, which makes Mom mad because she says it's such a waste, but she wasn't there so it didn't matter. Dad had cannelloni, which he always used to have whenever we went for Italian with Mom before Skinny came along, and I couldn't help thinking how great it would have been if only Mom had been there instead of Skinny Lynny.

"So who was your mysterious Sir Galahad who galloped in to give you a kiss?" asked Skinny Lynny. "Is he your boyfriend?" I wanted to slap her.

In my relief at getting Epona from James, I hadn't realized its implications, but as I relived the moments when James pressed Epona into my hand, another wave of despair swept over me.

James hadn't brought me my jacket; he had only given me Epona.

Which could only mean one thing.

James knew about the power of Epona. Had he used her to cause Moth more misery? And if James knew about Epona, how many other people at the yard knew, too?

CHAPTER 14

WHATEVER HAPPENED TO PEOPLE sleeping on Sunday mornings?" asked Drummer as I tugged him toward the field gate.

"It's an emergency; I'll explain on the way," I told him. After a sleepless night I had rushed to the yard early, hoping to catch James as soon as he arrived, but when I'd got there, Moth's tack was missing from the tack room: James had already gone riding. At least he was alone, I thought, checking all the other tack. I had to find him before anyone else arrived to find out whether my secret was safe. I couldn't face anyone else.

"What? No breakfast?" complained Drum as I flicked dirt from his back and tummy with a brush. "What *is* going on?"

"Shhh, just trust me on this," I said, tightening the girth. Fastening my riding hat, I led Drummer out of his stable and swung into the saddle, urging him along the drive and onto the bridle path. He snaked along from left to right, unwilling to go out alone and annoyed at being hurried.

"We have to find James and Moth," I shouted. "James knows all about Epona, and I need to talk to him about it before he tells the whole world."

"Oh!" said Drummer, straightening up immediately. "That's tricky!"

"Do you think?" I replied sarcastically. "I mean, what if he's told Catriona? What if everyone knows? And you know about my suspicions about him and Moth!"

"Everyone will want a piece of Epona," said Drummer, shuddering. "It doesn't bear thinking about—the whole world being able to talk to us. Hell on wheels! How come James knows, anyway?"

"He found her in my jacket pocket," I explained, "and brought her to me at *Pony Whispering Live!* after I left my jacket hanging up outside your stable."

"What nerve," grumbled Drummer, "going through your pockets."

I hadn't thought of that. What had James been thinking of, rummaging around in my jacket? Was there no limit to how low he would stoop? And I'd thought he was hot! Serious judgment error there, I thought.

"Where could they have gone?" I wailed. The bridle path forked off into four different directions with absolutely no clues about which path James and Moth might have taken.

"Shhh, quiet for a second," hissed Drummer. Lifting his head he sniffed the air. "I think they went this way," he said, heading for the right-hand path at a brisk canter. "Come on, we need to get a move on!"

We cantered through the path, which was rather overgrown. Twigs tugged at my sweatshirt, brambles caught on my jodhpurs, and Drummer cursed several times when branches whipped his legs.

"Are you sure they went this way?" I asked him. I could feel my heart thudding and I felt a bit sick. So many thoughts were whirling around my brain.

"Not really, but they're definitely in this direction. It's your turn to trust *me* on this!"

I had little choice; I didn't have a clue where to start. The bridle path opened out onto a hill and the countryside stretched before us, farmland crisscrossed by foot and bridle paths. Desperately, we both scanned the area, our eyes sweeping left to right and back again for signs of movement.

"There!" cried Drum, looking to the right where a field full of crops was bordered by woodland. I could just make out Moth's chestnut frame hammering toward the trees. James was wearing a red top—they looked like tiny models in a model farm.

"Come on!" yelled Drummer, bursting so suddenly into a canter, I was left gasping for breath and clutching his mane. "We'll catch Mr. Nosy yet!"

The wind tore tears from my eyes as Drum's canter turned into a gallop and we raced down the hill toward our quarry, turning the corner of the field at the bottom and thundering toward the chestnut figure topped with red. Daring to take one hand off the reins, I pushed Epona down deeper into my pocket. I couldn't imagine losing her now.

Drum was right; James had some nerve going through my jacket pockets—what had he been thinking? Did he go through everyone's gear in the barn? Not only did he treat Moth unkindly, I thought, he couldn't keep his

171

hands off other people's property either. I started to feel very angry. What a smarmy piece of work, all charm when it suited him and then going behind my back like that. Someone like that was bound to mistreat his pony. I'd give him a piece of my mind!

As we bore down on Moth, she suddenly saw us out of the corner of her eye and jumped around to face us, startled. I saw James stroke her neck, saw him look up and see us, his bewildered expression turn into one of understanding. He knew why we were desperate to catch up with him. When we came to an untidy halt, Drum kicking up dust and snorting, James and Moth facing us with Moth in her familiar stilted pose, James's face was completely unreadable. And then as we stood breathless before them, I couldn't think of anything to say. Where could I possibly start?

"Hi," said James.

"Hi," I replied. I didn't know what else to say now that I was facing him.

"Oh, get your act together, will you?" interjected Drummer, panting hard. "I risked windgalls and splints on my legs to get us here and all you can say is *hi!*"

"Umm, you brought Epona to me yesterday," I mumbled.

"Who?" said James, puzzled.

"The little statue you brought to *Pony Whispering Live!*" I explained.

"Ahhh, yes. That's an interesting little trinket you have there," James said, smiling. Was he smirking? How dare he?!

"Er, about Epona—" I started. I was ready to give James that piece of my mind I'd promised myself.

"Yes," interrupted James, "I was sorely tempted to keep it. Very handy. I always wondered how it would feel to be a pony whisperer, and yesterday, after discovering your little stone friend in your jacket pocket, I found out."

"You had no right to go through my pockets!" I shouted.

"That's more like it!" snorted Drum.

"Well, actually—" James began—he was remarkably calm for someone who had been found out.

I interrupted him. "Riffling through people's belongings…and, and…I know about you and Moth, too, don't try to deny it." There, I had said it, and about time.

"Hold on a minute!" James said angrily. "I merely picked up your jacket, which had fallen on the ground, and as I did so, a very funny thing happened; I heard voices—equine voices. I knew it couldn't be the jacket that allowed me to do that, so I had a look around and found Epona, as you call it. And good thing I did; otherwise, your *Pony Whispering Live!* would have been *Pony Whispering Dead Dodo!* And what do you mean about me and Moth?"

He was right about *Pony Whispering Live!* but I didn't want to hear it. I didn't know what I wanted anymore; I felt confused and embarrassed at being found out—and James was sitting on Moth, all calm and in control. I was no more a pony whisperer than I was the Queen of England and James was being maddening, denying anything was wrong with his relationship with Moth.

173

Thoroughly wound up, I launched a counterattack to deflect the accusations away from me.

"I know you don't treat Moth the way you should. She's scared of you, anyone can see that. What do you do to her when no one else is around?"

James's mouth fell open. That got him, I thought. He thought no one knew.

"I don't believe this!" exclaimed James. "You're the Pony Whisperer, you tell me! Tell me what Moth told you!"

There was an awkward silence. I couldn't say anything because Moth had told me nothing.

"You two need your heads banged together," sighed Drummer.

"Keep out of this!" I shouted.

"Don't be so rude!" James shouted back.

"Not you! I'm talking to Drummer!"

"You really shouldn't have accused James of going through your pockets," whispered Drum.

"You were the one who went on about it!" I replied.

"I didn't go on about anything!" James yelled. Moth stood with her head tall, her ears working back and forth, unnerved by all the shouting. James stroked her neck and crooned at her. "Easy girl," he whispered.

"Start again," Drummer sighed. "Go on, just take a deep breath and start again. I may have been a bit...er... sort of..."

"Wrong!" I hissed.

"Wrong about what?" asked James, thoroughly confused.

"Mmmm. More *misinformed*, I'd have said," Drummer admitted. "About the jacket and everything. By you," he added. I wanted to twist his little red ears.

I took a deep breath. "I think I owe you an apology," I started.

"Absolutely. Apology accepted," said Drummer.

"I'm not apologizing to you!" I cried.

"Make up your mind!" said James through gritted teeth.

"I was talking to Drummer!" I explained. "Drummer, *butt out!*"

"Oh, isn't that charming?!" retorted Drum and went into a sulk.

I turned to face James. "Yes, you!" I said. "I owe *you* an apology."

"So ungrateful..." muttered Drummer. I cuffed his mane. He was getting far too much above himself.

"It was really good of you to bring Epona to *Pony Whispering Live!*" I continued. "And you absolutely saved the day. Thanks."

"You're welcome," said James, his face breaking into an easy grin.

"I'm sorry I accused you of going through my pockets. I see now that I was mistaken." I could feel myself going red. Apologizing was so hard, but I had been totally wrong.

"But Moth *is* nervous," I went on, "you can't deny it. Why else would she behave like she does? She's wary of you and on her guard all the time, like she's afraid to do anything or have any sort of personality. Like she's scared

175

of people. You can't say she isn't. And she's the only pony who refuses to talk to me. I can't shut most of the others up. What do you do to her? How *can* you mistreat her?"

James put his head back and laughed. Far from being embarrassed at being found out, he thought it was *funny*!

"Do to her?" he repeated. "I could have explained if you'd only asked, instead of leaping to your own, very wrong and insulting conclusions. I'd never do anything to hurt Moth, not after what she's been through," James said. "Some pony whisperer you are!"

"I'm sweating a bit here, and I'll catch a chill unless you walk me about," Drummer complained, with his customary bad timing.

"Can we walk for a while? Drummer's sweaty," I explained. I felt very confused. It seemed that this day was down on the calendar as Pia Embarrassment Day. Big time. I was obviously getting the wrong end of every stick.

We both turned into the woods and as we walked through the trees, the ponies' hooves making soft, thudding noises on the leaf-covered ground, James told me Moth's story. How for several weeks he had visited the chestnut mare when she had been tethered near an old factory by travelers who didn't seem too concerned about feeding her regularly. How he had taken her hay to eat when she had eaten all the grass her tether allowed and was reduced to licking the soil around her—hay his friend Declan, Cat's brother, had got from his sister Cat, with her blessing. Even though they had told the authorities, nothing could be done as the travelers visited the mare and weren't exactly starving Moth. She wasn't a bad enough case for them to get involved.

And then James explained how one day, he and Declan had seen three youths tormenting her—two of them had been riding, her tether winding around the tree she was tied to, and the other had been hitting her with a stick, making her go faster. James sounded quite choked up as he relived it all and he stroked Moth's neck as if to reassure her it would never happen again.

"You should have seen the terror in her eyes," said James, his voice changing again to one full of anger. "She couldn't get away; she was trapped. For all I know, it might not have been the first time they had done it. We had to do something."

"So what did you do?" I asked him, blinking back the tears I felt pricking behind my eyes. Poor, poor Moth.

"We lost it a bit. Declan and I grabbed the one with the stick and laid into him—nothing serious," James said, grimly. "The others ran off before we could get to them."

"Shame!" I said. I meant it. "So how did you come to buy Moth?"

"Er, well, actually, Dec and I untied her and took her to the yard," explained James. "We got Cat to talk Mrs. Collins into helping us—not that she knew we'd taken her, she just thought she was mine."

"You mean you *stole* her?" I asked, incredulously, my jaw dropping. Not only was James a hot boy, but it seemed he had a hot pony, in the criminal sense. I was astounded.

"Yes. We couldn't leave her there, she was in a horrible state, and we were terrified the boys would return. But then I went to the travelers and bought her from them, explaining how she had been in danger and how I'd just taken her away to keep her safe. She's mine now, honestly! It was a little tricky explaining, and I paid more than she was worth, really, but she's more than made up for it. They weren't too bothered about her anyway. I sometimes wonder whether they engineered the whole thing, to get me to buy her!"

"How did you get the money?" I asked, my heart thudding. I almost didn't want to know. How could he get his hands on a stack of money on short notice?

"Oh, I was going to get a pony anyway. I persuaded my parents that Moth was the one," James said airily, like it was the easiest thing in the world. I imagined how that would have gone if I had been the one asking: "Oh, by the way, Dad, I've found a skinny pony I like. Can I have a giant wad of cash to pay for her?" I could imagine the answer I would have got. It seemed that James's family was anything but impoverished if they could buy a pony at the drop of a hat. Just how many more times could I be wrong today? It seemed I had to totally rethink all my ideas about James.

I was totally impressed—what a story! How could I ever have thought that James mistreated Moth? He had *saved* her. He was her *hero*. It seemed James made a habit of being a hero. I felt just awful having accused him of all sorts of things and I apologized again. He was really good about

178

it. What a relief knowing I could be friendly with him with a clear conscience—my heart suddenly felt all jumpy again and I felt myself sighing with relief that James wasn't a baddie after all. Could I be any more fickle? Feeling my face going red, I changed the subject.

"So you know the secret behind my pony whispering?" I said, sheepishly. James grinned at me.

"Yep!" he said. "You're a pretty cool customer."

"Well, it sort of took on a life of its own—everyone insisted I was the Pony Whisperer; I didn't actually claim to be one. And it's taken over my life—it's as though Epona's spell has turned me into a puppet, with everyone pulling on my strings. I just hope it all dies down now. You've no idea what it's like lying to everyone. I feel like such a fraud."

"Better than exposing Epona to everyone," James said.

"That's what Drummer says," I told him.

"It seems that Drummer says quite a lot of things," James said, pointedly.

"Hey!" said Drummer, forgetting he was sulking. "I am here, you know. I'll thank your boyfriend to keep his snotty remarks about me to himself!" I was glad James couldn't hear him. Drummer wasn't big on discretion.

"But do you think he's right—this time?" I asked, ignoring Drum.

"Yes," James said firmly. "Look, Pia." He turned in the saddle and looked at me earnestly. "Epona is a fantastic opportunity—I think you're obliged to help horses and ponies, really. If you gave her up, who knows how unscrupulous people would exploit the ability to communicate with equines? With you, the secret is safe. It's for the equine good!" he finished, dramatically.

"Are you sure?" I asked. James had no idea how good it was to hear someone else confirm my own thoughts. "It's fantastic to be able to help horses, like poor Seagull. But, you know, Moth won't talk to me. I've tried to talk with her, but she just refuses. No wonder—now I know her history, it's amazing she trusts anyone."

"She talked to me," said James, quietly, gently pulling Moth's ears. "When I realized Epona held the secret of communicating with horses, I so wanted to talk with Moth. And she spoke to me. You've no idea how great it was to hear her and listen to what she had to say. She was grateful to me for rescuing her. We had a long talk and I'm even more touched knowing that she wouldn't talk to you. Please don't give Epona up, Pia. I'd love to borrow her now and again to communicate with Moth, if you'll let me."

"Of course I will. I'm glad she spoke to you. I feel so ashamed at doubting you, James. Can you ever forgive me?"

"Nothing to forgive!" laughed James. "We'll make a pact—Epona and us against the world!"

"I was so relieved to get Epona back yesterday," I continued. "I was terrified Catriona might have found her. She'd waste no time in telling everyone I was a fraud. She hates me."

"Catriona's not bad; she's just a bit insecure," James confided. "She's got three older brothers so she has to fight to be noticed all the time at home. Getting Bambi was the best thing that ever happened to her."

"She's not very nice to me," I said. Clearly James liked Cat, and she had helped him with Moth so I didn't feel I could say anything too bad.

"She's just scared of your pony whispering title," said James. "Cat loves to be the center of attention because she never is at home, so it must be hard for her to watch everyone going to you about their ponies, to see the new girl taking center stage when she used to be the one everyone went to for advice."

"But I don't want to be there!" I wailed. "She can have the stage for all I care!"

"Give her Epona then!" James laughed.

I pulled a face. It seemed that Catriona and I were destined to be enemies, after all. Then something else occurred to me.

"James, what is it about Cat and Bambi? What's the big secret there? I know there's something, but Katy and Dee won't tell me, something about Bambi going back. Back where?"

"Nothing," mumbled James. I could tell he was lying. There was something.

"Are you sure? Or are you just not telling?"

"Well, it's up to Cat to tell you, not me."

And that's all I could get out of James. It seemed that Cat had kept his secret, and he was doing the same for her. Chivalrous, but annoying. I sensed it would have been pointless to push it.

That night in bed, I had all sorts of thoughts racing around my mind, keeping sleep at bay. It seemed that Catriona wasn't quite as hard as she wanted me to think she was, if I went by James's assessment of her.

How would I feel if someone new just came along and grabbed all the attention I had been used to getting, I wondered. And then I got a jolt because I realized that I was behaving exactly like Cat—but to Skinny Lynny. She'd come along and changed everything, and I hadn't given her a chance. I was behaving to Skinny just as Cat behaved to me. It gave me a weird feeling. Not good at all. I hadn't tried to get to know Skinny Lynny, just as Cat hadn't bothered to be friendly toward me. Which raised the big question—did I want to behave like Cat, or did I want to do things differently? It felt uncomfortable drawing parallels between my own behavior and that of Catriona. This was quite a day for rethinking things.

And there was one other thing I had to get sorted out. I had to tell Mom how much I disliked Graham—not actually because of *him*, but because of the way she changed when she was with him.

I'd had enough of twisting the truth. I thought I'd give being honest a go. See how that went. It wouldn't be easy, but it had to be done.

CHAPTER 15

WHAT ABOUT THIS ONE?" asked Mom.

I stared at the profile on the computer screen. We were onto our umpteenth profile on Mom's dating website and I was learning all sorts of things. They weren't necessarily things I wanted to learn, but after coming clean about Graham, I thought I'd better take an interest. No good just being negative, I'd decided, I had to put a positive slant on things. It had seemed to work.

Screwing up all my courage, I had told Mom how much I disliked her seeing Graham. It wasn't really him, I had said; it was the way she turned into a simpering little woman whenever he said anything patronizing and pompous—which was all the time! She had been mad at first and defensive, but then she admitted that she hadn't liked the person she seemed to turn into whenever she was with him either. Success! I had been worried she'd tell me to mind my own business, but instead she said she welcomed my constructive criticism and rather than me just complaining about Graham, that any new relationship had to be OK with me. That was a huge relief. I mean, if Mom was determined for another man to be in her life, it was nice to think she was thinking of me, too.

We talked for ages and Mom had told me that getting back into the dating scene had really boosted her confidence, which had taken such a knock when Dad had left her for Skinny Lynny. But then she'd realized that us being on our own wasn't so bad, and that she was finding out things about herself and getting stronger because of it. I didn't understand a lot of it but was thrilled to hear that Graham was getting his marching orders. I mean, I had said, surely she didn't have to settle for someone like Graham, and Mom agreed. She said she'd rather we were by ourselves than put up with someone who didn't want her to be herself—and she was still discovering who "herself" was.

So here we were, trawling the website for a Graham replacement. Or two. Or three, Mom had giggled. No sense in giving up her newfound freedom, she said, she just wanted to go out now and again, not jump into too much of a committed relationship. It was all music to my ears.

"So who would be your ideal sort of man, then?" I asked Mom. She thought for a moment.

"Well, I don't really know. I mean, I'm trying to keep an open mind. It's like Graham—he wasn't right for me, but he *might* have been. I wouldn't have known if I'd just dismissed his profile because I had thought he was too old. Also," she continued, scrolling down profiles, "I really need to just get back into the dating game so that I don't behave all the time like I did with Graham. I need to practice."

"Like the princess?" I asked.

"What do you mean?"

"The one who had to kiss a lot of frogs before she found her prince."

Mom giggled. "*Exactly!*" she said.

We found two profiles we liked the looks of and Mom got to work emailing them, telling me to go and see Drummer or something; she could do it herself! So I pedaled to the yard with Epona, as ever, safely in my pocket. It was unthinkable to see Drummer without being able to converse with him now. Life before Epona seemed like such a long, long time ago.

The sun was low in the sky as I made my way to the field where the ponies were grazing in their preferred couplets and groups. The red sun bathed the whole field in a beautiful soft golden light, and Drummer's coat was a fiery red, Moth's light chestnut coat was almost amber, and Bluey's black coat had an orange tint. Tiffany's golden coat gleamed like a newly minted coin and Bambi's chestnut patches were like flames. I couldn't see what color Mr. Higgins's coat was, but the buckles on his blue lightweight turnout rug glinted in the sunlight as he moved. No change there, I thought.

Seeing me walking across the field toward him, Drummer wandered over, Bluey following close behind.

"Hello, you," I said, rubbing Drummer's forehead and fishing out the tube of mints I had in my pocket. Drummer took one and didn't protest when I offered one to Bluey.

"How very kind!" cried Bluey, his gray lips brushing my palm gently as he took the mint, crunching it up noisily and exhaling minty breath.

185

"How's it going, then?" asked Drummer. "You know, life and all?"

"Not bad, actually," I told him.

"Still having trouble with your mom?"

"Not so much. She's got a lot of frogs to kiss, apparently."

"Whatever does it for her..." murmured Drummer, frisking my pockets for more treats.

"You getting on OK?" I asked Drum.

"Bambi and Tiffany are still not speaking to me—that's no big deal!" confided Drummer, rolling his eyes toward where the skewbald and the palomino were grazing cheek to cheek. Ponies were just like people, I thought. They had their friends, their arguments, their enemies. They made friends, they had quarrels, they had falling-outs. Maybe it was impossible to get along with everyone, however much you wanted to, whether you were a human or a horse. Whether you were Cat, Bambi, Pia, Drummer, Dolly, or Skinny Lynny. But did that mean you should stop trying? I wondered. And then I remembered something else.

"Hey, Drum, do you know what the big mystery is about Bambi?"

"Mystery? What are you talking about?"

"I keep hearing tidbits of conversation about Bambi going back and Cat not having a pony to ride. Do you know what that's about? Or are you bound by the code and unable to tell me?"

"Code? What code?" asked Drummer, wrinkling his nose.

"The code, the one that prevented you from telling me about Moth and whether James was treating her badly, you remember!" I cried. "And he isn't, by the way; I made a huge mistake."

"Oh, I made the code thing up."

"What?" I couldn't believe it. What was my pony like?

"Yeah, well, Moth doesn't really talk to me much; she's more pally with Tiffany so I just deceived you with that one. I can't believe you fell for it!" Drum shook his head to discourage a fly.

"You are the pits sometimes! I *said* you were making it up!" I told him. "So what about Bambi? What do you know?"

"How would I know? You know she doesn't talk to me."

I just *had* to get James to tell me, even though he'd refused before. There had to be a way to get him to spill the beans. Trouble was, I didn't think very straight whenever he was around. I went a bit fluttery and my head seemed to be filled with cotton wool. I wondered if that was how Mom felt when she went on a date with a new man. I hoped I didn't act like she had with Graham. I'd have to watch that.

"How's the pony whispering business?" Bluey asked me, politely.

"I'm playing it down," I told him. "I've had enough of being a horsey celeb. It's not a bit how I imagined it would be so I've decided I'm going to retire. I just hope it doesn't all fire up again when *Pony Whispering Live!* is aired. I'll still talk to all of you, of course," I added.

"Retiring, eh?" mused Drummer. "That'll be the day."

"I mean it, Drum," I said. "From now on it's just going to be something between you and me—and the other ponies here if they want to join in."

"And James!" Drummer reminded me.

"Mm, yes, I had said that he could be included, for Moth's sake."

My cell phone indicated that I had a message. Fishing it out of my pocket, I flipped it open. It was from James. My delight soon turned to gloom when I read it, and I groaned.

"What's up?" asked Drum.

"It's James; he says he's got me another pony whispering gig."

"Since when has he been your agent?" Drummer asked. He still hadn't forgiven James for discovering Epona in my jacket pocket, even if he had saved *Pony Whispering Live!* I realized I'd neglected to tell James of my retirement plans.

The ponies turned their heads—they'd heard the field gate creak as someone opened it and came into the field. Following their gaze I saw Sophie, Dee's mom, coming to get her beautiful liver chestnut, Lester. Or so I thought. She walked toward us and my heart began to sink.

"Pia, I wonder…" she began.

"Uh-oh," said Drummer, "here it comes. Retire, my tail!"

Sometimes, I just wish my pony didn't have the drop on me all the time. I mean, how does he *know* these things?

"I have a friend who's having awful trouble with her horse and I happened to mention you," Sophie went on.

"She'd be terribly grateful if you could spare a few moments to go over to her yard—I don't mind taking you—and see whether you can have a word. He's a dressage horse, comes from the South, very high-strung…" she went on and on telling me all about the problems her friend was having.

"Going to keep a low profile, eh?" chuckled Drum. I decided he ought to get himself a scarf bound with golden coins around his ears, set himself up in a tent, and call himself the Great Drumo, Fortune-Teller Extraordinaire!

"It's another case for the Pony Whisperer!" cried Bluey.

"Someone else is in need of your unique assistance," Bluey enthused.

"Only you can help; you can't say no, surely?" added Drummer, with more than a hint of sarcasm.

Oh, well, here we go again, I thought, my heart sinking. I could see that the retirement of the Pony Whisperer didn't seem to be an option—I couldn't expect to be able to talk with Drum and share a secret with James without some sort of payoff. There seemed to be no going back now.

COMING SOON...

The Pony Whisperer

TEAM CHALLENGE

"HEY, PIA," CALLED JAMES, sticking his head over Drummer's stable door, "lend us You-Know-Who for a bit, will you?"

"What's the problem?"

"I need to ask Moth why she's started to drop her hind legs over jumps, taking the poles with her. I bet it's something I'm doing wrong," James added. "It always is."

I handed James the little statue of a tiny stone woman sitting sideways on a tiny stone horse that I always, *always* have hidden safely in my pocket. It's with me whenever I go to the stable yard where I keep Drummer. Moth is stabled next door to Drum, and no one except James and I knows the secret of Epona—code name You-Know-Who—and we've both sworn to keep it that way!

"Thanks!" he said and disappeared to have a talk with his pony. That's right—a chat. Because even though her nose is missing and she's two-thousand-odd years old, Epona (are you ready for this?) has the power to let whoever is holding her hear what horses and ponies are saying and talk to them.

I know! When I found the ancient statue of the Celtic and Roman goddess of horses and heard Drummer talking to me, I could hardly believe it either. But because of Epona, and because I hadn't had the sense to keep what I discovered about the horses and ponies around me to myself, I had been proclaimed the Pony Whisperer, and all hell had broken loose. I'd helped horses and ponies that had problems, I'd upset people by telling them things they didn't want to hear, and I'd even been on TV—twice!

Since then, I've tried to live it down and escape the public eye because, believe me, being the Pony Whisperer may sound glamorous (I thought so too until it all got out of hand), but actually Epona got me into the sort of fixes I want to avoid these days.

Avoiding attention has not been one of my most successful ventures.

Of course, with Epona helping James I couldn't carry on the conversation I'd been having with Drummer, but as Katy and Bean chose that moment to lean on Drummer's stable door like cartoon twins, it was just as well. As Katy has red hair and is shorter than me and Bean is nothing like her, they don't look anything like twins, but you get where I'm coming from.

"Pia," announced Katy, shoving her hair off her face and puffing out her cheeks, "you and Drum have got to be in our team, haven't they, Bean?"

"Yeah, yeah, you've sooo got to be," agreed Bean, beaming at me. (Her real name is Charlotte Beanie, but everyone calls her Bean. With her height (tall), build (slim), and hair color (blond), she is the perfect match for her elegant palomino pony, Tiffany.)

I was delighted they wanted to include me as I still felt very much the new girl at the yard. Everyone else there had known each other forever, and although my Pony Whisperer title ensured I didn't stay out of the limelight, I didn't feel like I was really one of the gang. Drummer had been welcomed with open hooves by his fellow equines—apart from one, who I'll tell you about...

"We're taking the Sublime Equine Challenge," Katy announced, "and we just need you to complete our team of four."

"Yeah, we need someone to do the wild card," explained Bean. "Me and Tiffany are doing the show jumping—woo-hoo—and Katy and Bluey are our cross-country entry, of course!"

"I can't wait!" gushed Katy. "It'll be an opportunity to wear my new cross-country colors."

"What color are they?" I asked, teasingly. Katy has a thing, bordering on obsession, about purple, and her last cross-country shirt and matching skullcap cover would have made a Roman emperor envious. Her new colors were reputed to be even flashier.

When I'd first met Katy, I had been able to tell her—courtesy of Epona—that her chunky blue roan pony Bluey longed to go cross-country jumping. Katy was nervous, but Bluey's talent soon built her confidence. It was one of my pony whispering successes, before things had taken a downward turn.

"Any chance of starting from the beginning?" I asked them. For an answer, Katy shoved the latest *PONY* magazine under my nose and jabbed her finger on the full page ad that was headed:

ARE YOU READY FOR THE SUBLIME EQUINE CHALLENGE?

Yes, I thought, I definitely am. It was the start of summer vacation and I was looking forward to six weeks of being with Drummer, entering some shows, and going riding, especially with James, as often as I could. Did I mention that James is rather adorable? No? Well, he is. The trouble is, I'm not the only one who thinks so…

Katy shook the magazine impatiently at me. I read on.

"Sublime Equine, the new, up-to-the-minute equine wear specialists, are searching for the top all-around junior riding team in the country. Could that be you? Four riders under the age of sixteen must each compete in their chosen disciplines of Show Jumping, Cross-Country, Dressage, and the Wild Card Event, where anything goes! After regional qualifiers, the finals will be held at the jumping course in Hickstead at the famous National Jumping Derby meeting. All finalists will win a complete riding outfit from the new Sublime Equine Derby range. For full details on how to enter, go to www.sublime-equine/hickstead-challenge.com."

"Wow!" I said. "Drummer could do the jumping, I suppose. We're not very good at dressage or—"

"Not so fast!" interrupted Katy, her green eyes flashing. "Bean and Tiff are doing the show jumping—we just told you that, and I'm doing the cross-country—"

"Not that Tiff's great at jumping, but she's not bad," mumbled Bean, interrupting.

"And we thought you and Drummer would be fantastic at the wild card thingy-whatsit," Katy finished.

"Did you?" I replied, doubtfully. "What would we have to do?"

"That's just it," said Katy, waving her arms about in her best windmill impression. "Anything you like! Something wacky. Something different. You and Drum will be perfect!"

ABOUT THE AUTHOR

Janet Rising's work with horses has included working at a donkey stud, producing show ponies, and teaching both adults and children, with a special interest in helping nervous riders enjoy the sport, as well as training owners on how to handle their horses and ponies from the ground. Always passionate about writing, Janet had her first short story published when she was fourteen, and for the past ten years she has been editor of *PONY*, Britain's top-selling horsey teen magazine.